A HEART'S YEARNING

ROMANCING THE WEST

LINDA FORD

WILLOW CREEK, A TOWN IN THE
PORCUPINE HILLS OF ALBERTA. THE
YEAR—1887

*F*inn saw the blur of little feet, a billowing blue-flowered skirt, and a flash of blonde braids right in front of them. His breath knotted in his chest at the intrusion, at the knowledge that the ball of skirts and blonde hair was about to be trampled by his mule's hooves.

The child giggled as if she enjoyed every minute of it. And she would until it was too late.

A frantic call came from his right. "Stop, stop." A woman pursued the girl racing across the street in front of him.

Bill, his long-eared mule, skidded to a halt, his ears pointed forward.

The child made it to the steps of the trading post, now turned General Store, with the woman still in her wake.

The pair disappeared inside.

Bill's tail swished.

Finn's lungs released in a whoosh. He swiped his sleeve across his brow to wipe away the sweat. He tried to swallow, but a lump blocked his throat. Several seconds later, his brain began to function. "People ought to watch their children better'n that," he said to Bill. "If you weren't so smart someone might have been hurt." A shudder crossed his shoulders to think of the little girl running under Bill's hooves.

He continued toward the store and left Bill at the hitching rail. Finn ran his hand over his whiskers to smooth them, adjusted his battered hat—not that he cared what anyone thought of him. If he did, he wouldn't spend most of his time up in the mountains, avoiding contact with others except for the rare exception.

Life had taught him to be cautious about trusting people.

He paused at the steps, hoping the woman and child would leave before he went in. Words of warning and scolding burned at the back of his tongue. Someone ought to tell that woman how dangerous it was to let the child run heedlessly across the street. Not that he'd say anything. Nope. He would keep his opinions to himself. Or discuss it with Bill.

But the door didn't open and because it was a screen door, he could see the woman, the child now holding her hand, wandering around the interior.

Finn took a step back.

Bill snorted and nudged him.

"Don't push. I'll go in when I'm ready."

Bill gave a mule-sounding whinny which, at the moment, sounded a lot like mocking laughter.

Finn ground down on his teeth, grabbed the handle of the door, and yanked it open to step inside.

"How do, Finn," Burnsie called, his attention immediately leaving Finn as he turned back to the woman and child. "Got some nice books in. The little one might be in'erested."

"Thank you. Maybe another time." The woman turned, a bright smile on her face.

Finn forgot to breathe. Plumb forgot it was rude to stare. She was so beautiful it froze his mind. Chocolate-colored hair. Arresting green eyes. The face and smile of an angel. He mockingly reminded himself she had let a little girl almost run under the hooves of an animal, but the words were distant echoes.

"Sally, say good-bye to Mr. Burnsie."

The little girl gave a shy smile and mumbled, "Good-bye."

The woman glanced at Finn. Her eyes widened almost unperceptively and then she looked away.

He drew in a long quiet breath. And ignored the

feeling he'd been measured and found wanting. It was something he should be used to by now. But he wasn't.

The pair left the store. Through the screen, he saw them stop and talk to Bill. They both patted his neck. Bill looked ready to melt into a pool of butter. Crazy mule was a sucker for attention. Not that Finn didn't give him a goodly amount of it. After all, Bill was all he had for companionship. They often had long conversations, albeit rather one-sided.

"That's one of the new ladies in town," Burnsie explained even though Finn had not asked for an explanation. "Four of 'em, there is. They's opened a café across the street and they bake bread and goodies for sale. Hardworking bunch they is. But Miss Jenny Lyster, she's the purtiest by far."

A café and bakery? He might stop in and see what they offered. Not because he wanted to see Miss Lyster again and decide for himself if she was the "purtiest." No. Only because he had a hankering for homemade food and fresh bread.

But Burnsie's words hovered in Finn's mind. Hardworking? Did that include Miss Lyster? Was she beautiful and industrious? He tried to sort out his fleeting impressions of her, but they were all tangled in confusion.

Burnsie continued. "Kinda figgered you'd be showin' up soon for supplies. Good thing too. Got a letter here says it's important. 'Deliver immedit'ly.'" Burnsie studied the missive a moment then turned his attention back to Finn. "Been wonderin' who I could send out to find ya."

Finn took the letter Burnsie handed him and stuck it in his pocket. Who would be contacting him? And why? Ah, well, the answers could wait. He would read it in private. He ordered the supplies he needed. "I'll pick 'em up when I'm ready to leave town."

He didn't say when that would be and Burnsie didn't need to ask, because Finn's habit was to ride in, get supplies, and ride out the same afternoon. He didn't see why this day would be any different.

"The food over there any good?" He tipped his head in the general direction he expected the new café was located.

"The best."

"Think I'll mosey over and get a feed."

"You do that. You won't be disappointed." Burnsie was already getting together the items Finn had ordered.

Finn returned to the step.

Bill's ears flicked back and forth.

"Yeah. I saw it. Don't be expecting it every day."

Bill pulled back his lip.

"And no back talk."

Bill looked away. Sometimes that mule was a tad bit too human-like. Of course, it made up for lack of companionship in Finn's life.

Finn stepped into the street. "Come on, long ears, I'm going across the street for a meal. Or do you want to wait here?"

Bill was on his heels, breathing down his neck as they crossed to the café. The freshly painted sign read *New Café and Bakery. Good Home Cooking.*

He left Bill in front of the establishment and pushed open the door.

Scents of home and good food assailed him. Bread, displayed in the case, gave forth an aroma that made his stomach growl. Added to that, cinnamon and other spices and a savory smell of dinner were about enough to make a man weak in the knees.

To his surprise, most of the tables were full of men. A glance was all he needed to determine they were mule skinners, their usual boisterous and raucous talk subdued by their surroundings.

Spying an empty table across the room, close to the corner, Finn sauntered over and parked himself on a chair that had his back to the wall. He could see the goings on from there and not get all jittery that someone might be approaching from behind.

Huh. Maybe he had been alone too long. He was getting a mite suspicious about others.

A woman crossed the room toward him. She was pretty enough, he supposed, with brownish hair. Brown eyes. "Can I get you something? Coffee, pie, dinner? It's roast venison. Hilda's special recipe. And all the fixings."

His stomach answered loudly.

To her credit, the woman acted like she hadn't noticed.

"Dinner sounds good. And coffee. Please."

"Coming right up."

The men around him sat with knife in one hand, fork in the other. Waiting for their meals.

Through the open doorway that revealed a kitchen, he saw two children sitting at a table while three women hustled about preparing the food. He recognized the little girl as the one who had scampered across the street. Where was Miss Lyster? After Burnsie's comments about the girl being hardworking, he'd expected to see her bustling around the kitchen. Or the dining room. Making herself useful.

You'll never be appreciated for just being. Best you learn to be useful. The words came in his foster father's voice. The comment was usually followed with something more. *You want a home, you best keep your attitude to yourself. No one wants an angry, rebellious boy.* He'd heard those words the first time when he was seven, newly orphaned and taken in by the Moores. He vowed he would be useful and hide his feelings. His decision had ensured him a home until he was fourteen.

Why was he recalling that particular incident now? Maybe because he was thinking of the ladies being hardworking and work always reminded him of Mr. Moore.

He pushed aside the memories. They served no purpose.

Besides, he was thinking about Miss Lyster ...or rather, trying not to think of her.

7

The big blonde woman went to the back door, opened it, and called out.

Finn couldn't make out what she said but Miss Lyster hurried in, carrying a basket of what looked like fresh greens. She washed at the back door and grabbed two plates of food and carried them out to one of the tables.

Finn almost laughed at the way the bunch of men sat up straighter and watched her progress in and out of the kitchen carrying plates to the tables. Not that he could blame them. She was a treat to watch. Not only was she pretty as a newly picked bouquet of wildflowers, she moved like a deer—graceful and quick.

Might be enough to overlook any faults she might have, though he doubted there were any. He ground down on his teeth. Good thing he had no interest in developing a relationship. He'd be back at his mountain cabin later this afternoon. And enjoying his solitude.

Two of the other young ladies helped carry out the plates and one of them put a full plate before him. He thanked her and tucked into the food. It was excellent and there was a generous amount of potatoes, meat, gravy, and turnips. He wondered where they had gotten the vegetables, which were scarce this time of year. They must have had Burnsie ship them in.

Each summer, he grew a few things for his own use, and as well, foraged for roots and berries in the woods, but apart from some tender greens he'd picked along the riverbank the other day, his vegetables were long gone.

He listened to the conversation around him as he ate.

"There's four of 'em," one man said. "None married." He leered in the direction of the kitchen where the women could be seen working.

"Tha's not possible. There's two kids. I seen 'em. So did you."

The first man nodded. "Yup. They's orphans. Hear tell one of the gals is raising them."

Finn let his gaze circle the room. For men who were consuming hearty meals, they certainly had a hungry look to them. Nothing to do with food, he knew.

"Which one is prettiest, do ya think?" one of the men asked.

"I favor the one who has the kids."

"Nah. She's kind of plain. That one—" He jabbed his thumb in the direction of the woman who was cutting pies— "the big blonde. Now there's a woman who could help a man."

"They has names," another said.

"How do you know them?"

The man chuckled. "I asked. The blonde is Mrs. Meyer—Hilda Meyer. She's a widow, I hear."

Several men, recognizing the German name, sighed with what Finn knew was homesickness.

"The one with the kids is Miss Morton—Delcie Morton."

Finn was sure that every pair of eyes shifted to the woman being named.

"That pretty little thing scraping the plates, be Miss Fisher. Laura Fisher. Don't know much about her."

As if controlled by the same master, eyes shifted to the woman in question.

"And the one by the table?"

Finn knew her name. Miss Lyster. Jenny Lyster.

The informant gave her name. "She's awfully pretty."

"Too pretty for her own good," one of the men commented.

"Me pa always said a real purty woman don't make a good wife."

Several men grunted agreement.

Finn studied Miss Lyster. Didn't seem fair to judge her based solely on her looks. Now if they'd seen her with the child…

He knew that was unfair, as well. Children got away from even the best parents. He'd reserve judgment.

He grinned at his foolishness. He'd soon be up on his mountain and forget about the women that had so many men talking marriage.

Marriage wasn't for him. He'd made that decision a long time ago.

The one known as Miss Fisher carried a pot of coffee from table to table and refilled cups.

The other three brought out pieces of pie for each diner.

Finn lingered over his meal even after the others had departed. The food was too delicious to eat in a rush.

He lifted his cup, discovered it was empty, and put it down again. Content with the meal, he leaned back and patted his stomach. His pocket crackled. He remembered he had a letter and pulled it out. He broke the seal with his thumbnail, unfolded the sheet of paper and glanced at the signature. *Ethel.*

The name triggered a flood of memories. Memories he thought he had eradicated from his mind. He did his best to shove them back into oblivion and read the contents of the letter.

Huh? Surely this was a mistake.

But he read it again a second and a third time and the message remained the same.

He pressed the back of his hand to his forehead.

How could she ask him such a thing?

JENNY TURNED at the sound of rattling paper. She saw the man at the far table clutching a letter in one hand and pressing his other hand to his forehead. It was the man she'd seen at the store. The one Burnsie called Finn. The name was wild sounding. Matched the man perfectly. His golden brown hair was to his collar in a tangle of curls. He had a beard the same color as his hair. Impossible to tell his age, but she knew enough about hiding one's feelings to know this man was doing exactly that.

Something about that knowledge tugged at her heart.

Without giving herself time to reconsider, she grabbed the coffeepot and went to his table. "More coffee?"

He nodded though she wondered if he truly heard her.

She filled his cup. Considered returning to the kitchen but instead, she sat in the chair across from him.

His eyes widened. Nice eyes, she thought. Golden brown like his hair.

"Do you mind if I join you?" She knew he could hardly refuse seeing as she was already seated. Unless he had no manners at all.

He shrugged, his eyebrows rising toward his curly hair. "Seems you already have."

She grinned at his reply. "Allow me to introduce myself. Miss Lyster. Jenny Lyster. I am one of the four women who own and operate this establishment."

He nodded. "Finn Johnson's my name." He offered no more information and she understood he wouldn't.

They studied each other without speaking. What did he see? A young woman too pretty to be of any use? Those were the words that had turned her life upside down and sent her out west with the other ladies. Not that she regretted the trip. "We've only been here a short time." She couldn't imagine why she thought he'd be interested nor why she felt the need to tell him. "It's a beautiful country. I have asked to be in charge of the garden. We'll grow lots of vegetables so we can serve nice meals throughout the winter."

The only sign he gave that he listened was his unblinking study of her.

"But I want to make the garden beautiful as well as practical."

"Huh."

She couldn't decide if it was a questioning sound or a dismissive one though it made little difference. For some reason, she couldn't stop talking.

"I've been bringing in wildflowers and planting them." She sighed. "Not all of them are surviving."

He nodded. "Not easy to pull things out by their roots and replant them. It's not the same as being where they started."

She mused on those words a moment. "I think the same could be said about people." Then realizing he might think she meant she'd never be happy at Willow Creek, she added, "Sometimes being moved is better. In my garden, the plants will get watered, weeded, and tended very well."

"Guess that would work." He looked at the letter he held. "Though sometimes the plants are neglected. Or put in the wrong place."

She shifted her gaze to the letter and recalled why she had joined him. And it wasn't to talk about gardening. "Bad news?" She tipped her head toward the page in his hand so he would know what she meant.

His gaze slowly came to her and in the depths of his eyes she saw a vast longing. Recognized it as an echo of how she sometimes...all right... often...felt. A desire for understanding, sympathy, worth. Her heart responded with an understanding of the familiar emotions.

"Is there is anything I can do?"

He blinked, and whatever she thought she'd seen was gone. He folded the letter and carefully slid it into his breast pocket. "There's nothing you or anyone can do."

She expected him to hurry away but he sat there, his hands cradling his cup of coffee. Strong hands. The sort of hands that could do hard work. Would they be gentle or harsh?

When he didn't make a move to leave, she asked, "Where do you live? What do you do?"

"In the mountains. I hunt and trap and prospect."

"For gold? I heard there were traces of gold in the mountains. Have you found any?"

"No." He gave a fleeting grin. "Truth is I haven't looked very hard."

She chuckled. As much at his sudden hint of humor as his admission. "Why?"

"Maybe it's too much work."

From the tone of his voice, she guessed that wasn't the reason. "I'd say you're a man who isn't afraid of hard work."

The sound that came from his throat might have been a chuckle. It rumbled from some place deep within him.

"Nope. It ain't hard work that scares me. It's fickle people."

Again, Jenny felt that unspoken connection between them. "There are people you can trust. Like my friends." She watched Hilda taking bread from the oven. The aroma filled the building, promising good things, offering home and friendship.

She turned back to the man at the table—Finn Johnson. But something at the window arrested her attention before her gaze reached his. She gasped and pointed.

Finn followed the direction of her finger and scrambled to his feet.

2

$\mathcal{F}$inn glowered at Bill with his nose pressed to the window. Never could keep the animal tied up. He could untie knots faster than Finn could knot them. "My mule. He's got a mind of his own." Perhaps he should thank the animal for interrupting. What was he doing talking to a young lady? He well remembered the last time he had done so.

Just as he remembered how it had turned out.

It wasn't something he cared to repeat.

"I'm coming," he groused, though he knew Bill couldn't hear him. He paid for his meal, thanked the ladies, bought a loaf of fresh bread, and left the diner. "Come on, long ears." He wouldn't be returning to his cabin tonight. They paused at the store to collect his purchases. He stowed them in Bill's saddlebags then made his way to the river and chose a campsite.

He could cook over a fire. Or he could take his

meals at the new diner. That sounded more appealing. From what he knew so far, the food was excellent. No point in him surviving on beans even if the fresh bread would help them go down easy.

Bill sank down and got comfortable. The mule wasn't so stupid after all, Finn allowed, and he sank down too, his back to a tree. He drew out the letter and stared at the words.

Ethel had a son. Eddie. Edward Hankins. He needed a home. She was counting on Finn to give him one. He didn't read the rest of the letter again, finding the words too upsetting.

Finn rocked his head back and forth. "Can't do it," he muttered.

Bill sighed, as disinterested as the bug crawling across the ground.

Finn folded the letter carefully and put it back in his pocket. He couldn't take care of a boy. Why did Ethel think he could? Or would? Especially after the way she'd so firmly dismissed him. *You have nothing to offer someone like me.* Of course it was true. He was an orphan. Good only for doing whatever work needed doing. So why did she now think he had something to offer her son? It made no sense.

Restlessness made his legs twitch. A hike up a steep mountain would ease them but instead, he sat near a town, watching people come and go.

Slowly an idea took hold. Surely one of them would be interested in taking in a boy. He just had to find the right person. He shifted so he could see the dusty street traversing the length of town. And also anyone moving about in that general area. It wasn't long until someone came into view.

Miss Lyster scurried across the road and into the store. A few minutes later, she came out carrying something and disappeared behind the café. To her garden?

She'd said she wanted it to be beautiful as well as practical. What did that mean?

He might like to have a gander at her garden. A better idea than sitting here musing about a boy needing a home.

"I'm going for a walk," he said to Bill. "You stay here and behave yourself."

The mule looked away as if he liked the view from where he lay.

Finn pushed to his feet and sauntered down the trail, crossed the road, and angled toward the bakery. The garden filled up the empty lot beside the café. Neat little rows of struggling baby plants that he recognized. Lettuce, beans, peas, carrots, potatoes, all newly emerged and wind battered.

To the back were little sprouts that he guessed would soon be vines. Likely squash and pumpkin.

Against the building he saw more plants, wilted from having been dug out and transplanted. He stared at them a long while and thought about his and Miss Lyster's discussion about being torn up by the roots and planted elsewhere.

"The wind makes it hard to get the plants established."

He'd been aware of her watching him and then approaching, though he'd given no indication of it.

"They need some protection."

"Trees would help, but I can't wait for them to grow."

"You could build a fence. A good solid fence would block the wind and protect your garden."

She stared at him.

"A board fence about six feet tall. Posts would have to be set firmly so the wind wouldn't topple it."

He couldn't have explained to save his life why he was offering suggestion after suggestion. He was a solitary mountain man who seldom conversed with anyone. Unless you counted Bill, and few people would. But yet, he rattled on as if it was his normal behavior.

Miss Lyster leaned forward. "That would work." Her smile faded and she settled back on her heels. "But I don't think I can build a fence. I don't know how."

"I'm having to stay in town a few days." He had no way of knowing when the boy would arrive, but from the contents of the letter he guessed Eddie was on his way. "I could do it for you." How had he gone from making suggestions to offering to help? It was like someone had taken over his mouth without his permission.

Her eyebrows drew together. "I can't afford to pay you."

That stranger using his mouth spoke again. "I'd settle for some meals." He held his breath, wondering how she would respond to his unusual offer. Of course, she had no way of knowing how unusual it was. She wouldn't know that he didn't care to spend time around others.

She tapped her fingers against her forearm. "I'm agreeable, but I have to check with the others. Come on in and I'll introduce you." She headed for the back door.

Finn hesitated. Now was the time to make some excuse that he had changed his mind. Perhaps say he'd forgotten something important he had to do. Namely get back to his cabin and his solitude. But Ethel's letter forced him to stay and so he sauntered after her. As if he belonged in her world. Not that she was suggesting he did. Nor did he expect she meant that. But one thing he knew, for a man like him, his only value was in what work he could do. Like building a fence.

He stopped inside the kitchen and yanked his hat off, clutching it in both hands and pinning it to his chest.

Three ladies stopped what they were doing. Making supper, he surmised. One rolled out pie dough. One poured batter into cake tins. Another peeled potatoes.

Two children helped. The little girl carried potatoes to the cupboard to be peeled. The boy, slightly older, scoured out a cooking pot.

"Everyone." Miss Lyster's voice drew five pairs of curious eyes to her. "This is Mr. Johnson." She introduced the women. He already had their names figured out from the conversation in the dining area. Mrs. Meyer, the big blonde woman. Miss Fisher, the quiet, dark-haired woman who eyed him up with harsh judgment. He knew the look. She'd been hurt by a man. Just like he'd been hurt by a woman. Miss Morton, who wore a look of warning as the children clung to her.

Miss Lyster introduced the children. "Kent is six. His sister, Sally, is four."

The women murmured greetings and Miss Morton had the children say how-do.

Miss Lyster continued. "He says a fence is needed to protect the garden. Says he'll build it in exchange for meals. What do you think?"

The women's study of him grew more intense. He held his ground without flinching although a twinge started in his heels. He should never have offered. He could, even now, say he'd changed his mind. To his confusion, he discovered he didn't want to.

"Not every meal," he said. "I'd be happy with one a day." The rest he could manage on his own. After all, he'd been doing so for a very long time.

It was Mrs. Meyer who spoke. "Vould you mind vaiting outside vhile ve discuss this?" Maybe she wasn't long in this country. Her w's came out sounding like v's. Or maybe she would always retain an accent. Not that it mattered one way or the other to him. There were far more important things to his way of thinking.

His thoughts were getting all confused. It was time to leave. He fled out the door and made it as far as the edge of the garden and could not go any farther. He had to wait in town. Somehow he had to let Ethel know she must figure out some other solution for her son. But Eddie would be traveling alone, and he couldn't abandon the boy even though he'd never met him. Besides, the idea of getting a hot meal every day stopped him in his tracks. His mental arguments went round and round leaving him slightly dizzy. He made up his mind.

He could build a fence, enjoy some decent cooking, and keep his mouth shut. How hard could that be? Especially for someone like him who had lived alone for...was it really eight years since he'd left the place he'd considered home from the time he was orphaned?

* * *

JENNY FACED the curious questions of the others.

Who is this man? How do you know him?

Jenny explained he'd eaten dinner at the café. They all remembered him.

Laura Fisher, the most wary one apart from Jenny herself, asked, "Why is he prepared to stay around here? Doesn't he belong someplace?"

"I truly can't say but—" She told them of his letter. "It seemed to surprise him. Perhaps that has something to do with it. But it seems to me the important thing is we won't have vegetables if I can't grow a garden. A sturdy fence would help."

The others murmured acknowledgement of this fact. Without vegetables they wouldn't be running a café. At least not the sort they envisioned.

The business was Hilda's idea and she made the decision. "It seems ve need a fence and ve have a man villing to build it for us. Ve vill feed him in exchange. But if he does not act the vay a man should act, I vill chase him away vith my own two hands."

Jenny chuckled. She had no doubt that Hilda would do exactly that.

Kent tugged at Delcie's sleeve. "Auntie Delcie, is that man going to stay here?"

"No dear, but he will eat here." Delcie's narrow-eyed look informed Jenny that she didn't care to have the man lingering about. Jenny understood her caution concerning men. A man she'd trusted had kidnapped the children. Delcie hoped to start over here without worrying that it might happen again. Yes, they all had their reasons for moving west.

Sally's eyes widened. Jenny hoped she didn't see a spark of mischief. Sally often ran headlong into trouble and managed to keep all of them on their toes.

Jenny rocked her head back and forth. "Look at us. Four marriageable young women in a part of the country where there are ten men to every woman and all of us set on never marrying. What a disappointment we must be to the male population."

The others laughed but looked away, each thinking of their own reason for such a decision.

"Go inform the man," Hilda said. "Bring him in so ve can all have a better look at him. I vill give him coffee and cookies."

Jenny hurried outside. She glanced around. Had he left? Changed his mind? Why should she be disappointed? It wasn't like she didn't know she shouldn't trust a man. Not only had her experience taught her that, but so had that of the others. And yet, she'd thought this man was different. Why? Because he was a mountain man? It was hardly reason enough.

A movement caught her eye and she saw him sitting cross-legged on the ground, twisting a blade of grass between his fingers.

She made her way toward him.

His head turned her direction, his eyes shadowed by his hat, his whiskered face revealing nothing. What was he hiding?

She made herself stop trying to guess who he was and why he chose to live the way he did. None of that mattered. "We are in agreement that in return for building a fence, you may eat your meals free of charge in the café."

He rose to his feet in one swift movement. "Ma'am, I hope I don't disappoint."

She grinned. "I could say I hope our meals don't disappoint."

He tipped his head but not before she saw the

flicker of amusement and a teasing smile. "I don't think that is likely."

"Hilda would like to give you coffee and cookies."

He hesitated a moment before he replied. "I accept."

Inside the kitchen, Mr. Johnson sat across the table from the ladies, a cup of coffee and plate of cookies before him. He seemed unaware of their curious study.

"Mr. Johnson, tell us about yourself," Hilda said.

He swallowed back a large gulp of coffee. "First of all, I prefer to be called Finn."

Sally giggled. "You a fish?"

Delcie hushed the child but Jenny noticed that Mr. Johnson—Finn—appeared more amused than offended. Though she might be reading more into the way the skin at the corners of his eyes crinkled than she should.

"Why is that?" Laura's words brought them back to his request to be addressed as Finn. Her tone conveyed a good deal of suspicion, as if wondering what secrets the man hid behind his name.

"Just like it better'n Mr. Johnson."

Jenny wondered if any of the women would offer their Christian names, but none of them did and she wasn't about to be the first though it would feel awkward to call him Finn and have him address her as Miss Lyster.

"What do you want to know about me?" His words held a world of caution.

Jenny understood there were things he wasn't about to reveal and wondered what they were.

"Who are you?" Delcie asked, her gaze brushing the two children. She wasn't going to let anyone near them who might pose a risk.

"A mountain man. I don't come to town often and don't usually hang about, but I'm waiting for something."

"What's a mountain man?" Kent asked.

Finn's gaze softened as he turned to the boy. "It means I live up in the mountains mostly by myself. Oh, and my mule, Bill." He glanced out the window as if checking for his animal. "Surprised he isn't wandering around looking for me."

"Doncha keep him tied up?"

"No point. He can untie knots."

Kent's eyes widened. "Truly?"

"Truly. Maybe I'll show you."

Sally's eyes flicked from one to the other as she took in the conversation. It was hard to know what was going through that pretty little head.

Delcie pulled both children to her side. "Kent will be staying here with me." Her face was set in warning.

"Sorry, ma'am. I meant no harm."

"What do you do in the mountains?" Kent asked.

"Hunt, fish, look for gold." Finn downed his coffee and ate the last cookie. "Now if you will excuse me, I will see what I need for a fence." He headed for the door.

"I'll help." Jenny followed him outside. "I hope my

friends didn't offend you. They have their reasons for being cautious."

"No offense taken."

His dismissive tone triggered a protest, a desire to know why he was so reclusive. "I suppose you have your reasons for being cautious as well."

He shrugged. "We all have a past. Even a young thing like you, I suspect."

A young thing! Like she wasn't capable of...of being grown up and having an opinion, a mind of her own. "How young do you think I am?"

His chuckle was soft, mocking. "I might spend my days alone, but I know not to guess a woman's age."

"I'll have you know I'm eighteen years old."

He shrugged. "A young thing, like I said."

She was getting a little annoyed. "Spoken like an old man. Which you aren't. I'd guess you to be—" She deliberately studied him hard. "Oh, maybe twenty-five or bordering thirty."

He shrugged again. "You could be right."

"You aren't going to tell me? That's not fair. I told you."

"Miss Lyster, I am an old man compared to you in more ways than you can imagine." He stopped at the edge of the garden. "I suggest you build the fence here to give you the best protection. I'll pace it out and then you'll know what you need."

He'd changed the subject, so she let it go. But it didn't stop her curiosity. Not that it really mattered one way or the other. He'd build them a fence and go back to his mountain.

She'd tend her garden and help with the cooking and baking. It was all she wanted after the way Isaac Stanley had treated her. Or did she mean how his father had treated her? It didn't matter which she blamed the most. They were no longer a part of her world. The memories belonged in the life she'd left behind.

One didn't have to retreat to a mountain to find escape. Moving west and starting over with friends served the same purpose.

She followed Finn as he paced out the fence and muttered under his breath. He stopped at the far corner.

"I know what is needed for materials." He listed them off. "Burnsie might have the things in stock or he might have to order it." He stared past her toward the mountains. Was he longing to be gone? He brought his gaze to her. "Do you want me to go see Burnsie and ask?"

Jenny realized he meant they had to get supplies. How much would it cost? With their pooled resources the women had been able to purchase the building and make the necessary changes for the business, but it didn't leave a lot left over. However, the others had given permission for the fence, so she would proceed.

"I'll go with you to the store."

They crossed the dusty street and went inside.

Burnsie greeted them. If he found it strange to see

the two of them together, he hid it well. Though when Finn asked after fencing materials, Burnsie eyed him hard.

"You're buildin' a fence? Up on the mountain? Figure to keep your mule contained?"

"It's not for me," Finn said.

"It's for my garden," Jenny added.

Burnsie blinked. His mouth fell open and he stared a moment before he closed it so he could talk. "Finn's building you a fence? He's stayin' in town? Well, I'll be a—"

"Waitin' for somethin'," Finn mumbled.

He'd said that before. What could he be waiting for? The tone of his voice caused her to think it was something he wasn't anxious to get. She wished she felt free to ask him about it, but it wasn't any of her business.

They exited a short time later carrying a post-hole auger and with Burnsie's promise to deliver the needed posts he had in store.

Back at the garden, Finn began to dig a hole, his legs braced wide, his arms and shoulders bulging with the effort.

Jenny needed to know how to build a fence. The knowledge might come in handy in the future. After all, one never knew where life would lead her. She'd certainly not foreseen the circumstances that brought her to Willow Creek. She continued the mental excuses even as a part of her brain mocked her. She wouldn't likely ever have to build a fence. That wasn't why she watched so carefully.

No. It was simply good to watch a man at work. Willingly doing something to help her. No obligation or expectation other than three meals a day.

She spun around and strode toward the house. He might well be just like Isaac Stanley and his father. They'd seem kind and good in the beginning. She'd learned her lesson and wasn't about to trust a man— any man—for more than the work he'd offered to do.

3

_____

inn's breath eased out as Jenny headed for the house. As long as she watched him, his nerves jangled along the surface of his skin. What did she want? What did she see? Besides a scruffy mountain man. What she couldn't see was the stone encasing his heart from years of shutting people out. It was what aged him beyond his twenty-four years. Having her nearby made him acutely aware of the cold hollowness of that heart.

Her sudden gasp jerked his attention to her and then past her to his wayward mule.

He should have known Bill would come looking for him. Not that Bill gave Finn so much as a glance. No, the crazy animal had somehow managed to get behind Miss Lyster without her noticing and pressed his nose into her neck.

Finn grinned. That unexpected cold nose must

have given the gal quite a fright.

He hurried toward the pair. "Bill, behave yourself." He tried to push the mule away, but he refused to budge. "I'm sorry. I apologize for Bill's lack of manners. Did he scare you?"

She backed away. Bill stretched his neck trying to reach her as Finn pushed on him, vainly attempting to persuade him to leave. She wiped the back of her neck.

"Startled me a little." She watched the struggle between man and beast. A grin replaced her surprise and then peals of laughter rang out. She lifted her hand, opened her mouth as if trying to explain what was so funny, but she couldn't get a word out for laughing.

Finn leaned back on his heels and grinned, knowing he and his mule must be quite a sight. Him pushing. Bill immovable as a mountain boulder. He didn't mind that Miss Lyster found it amusing. In fact, he liked that he had made her laugh. He might be tempted to do silly things just to hear her. And see her. Her eyes crinkled, shining like a pair of those green gems. For the life of him, he couldn't think what the name was.

Bill rocked his head back and forth and made his odd whinny sound. Laughing with her, which served to make her laugh harder.

The animal pushed by Finn, stepping on his foot. On purpose, Finn knew. Bill pressed his head to Miss Lyster's shoulder.

She gave one more giggle than scratched the side

of Bill's head. "Sorry for laughing, but if you could have seen the look on both your faces."

Finn couldn't keep the pleased grin off his face. "Glad to be a source of amusement."

Her smile faded. Her eyes narrowed and she studied him. "I can't tell if you're all right with me laughing at you or if you're being sarcastic. I have no wish to offend you."

"Ma'am, you did not offend me."

"Ma'am?" She jammed her hands to her hips, forcing Bill to shift to one side. "First of all, it's miss and secondly, it's Jenny. That's my name. Jenny." She huffed out the words.

"Yes, miss. But I wouldn't be so bold." Besides, using her given name was like pounding a chisel to the shell of his heart. Far too friendly. Too dangerous. Threatening his boundaries.

Her eyes flashed. Only it wasn't with amusement this time. She studied him. Was about to say something when young Kent raced from the house.

"A donkey. Can I have a ride?"

"It's a mule," Finn corrected.

Kent didn't let that divert him. "Can I have a ride?"

"His name is Bill, and you best ask him."

Kent touched Bill's head. "Can I? Huh? Please."

Miss Lyster gave Finn a look of such pleading that he couldn't have refused her a trip to the seashore on Bill's back if she'd asked. But she only wanted Kent to have ride. He spoke softly to Bill. "Boy wants a ride." Then bent over and lifted Kent to Bill's back.

The boy grinned widely. He was a happy child despite being an orphan. Just a little younger than Finn had been when he lost his parents. But at least Kent had Miss Morton and the other ladies to bring him up. He wouldn't be forced to become a servant and learn to keep his thoughts and feelings to himself.

Finn glanced toward the house. Why wasn't Miss Morton rushing from the door, warning Finn to stay away from the boy? But there was no sign of her, so he continued to give Kent a ride.

Finn didn't need a rope to lead Bill around the yard. The mule followed, treading carefully as if aware he carried a child, precious cargo.

At first Miss Lyster walked at Bill's other side, as if to make sure the child was safe. Then she fell back.

Finn's gaze went past Kent to where she stood with a pleased smile. The affection on her face was as plain to read as the new sign above the café. He didn't know how to assess her. He'd judged her for letting the little girl dash across the street. Even judged her a tiny bit for not being in the kitchen helping with dinner though she had come and helped when asked. He'd seen her keenness for the garden and the evidence of her hard work. And now her fondness for the child. Not even her own. No doubt, in the time it would take to build the fence, he would see more of her and who she was.

What did it matter? And yet it did. But he wasn't ready to think why. Or at least to admit the reason to himself.

They returned to where they'd started. "Time to get down, young Kent," he said.

"Aww."

"Mr. Johnson has work to do." Miss Lyster spoke gently but firmly. Kent must have known the tone, for he nodded and allowed Finn to lift him down.

"Thank you for the ride." He patted Bill and Finn grinned to think the gratitude was to the mule. As well it should be. Finn led Bill from the yard and wrapped his lead rope around the hitching rail in front of the café. Not that Bill would stay there unless he wanted to. As if to remind him of that fact, Bill grabbed the end of the rope and flipped it over the rail.

"Stay there and behave yourself. I got work to do."

Bill pretended a great interest in something in the distance.

The boy went to where Finn had been digging a hole and squatted down.

"Kent wants to watch you." Miss Lyster studied Finn. "He is surrounded by women. It might be good for him to be around you for a bit."

Miss Morton rushed to the door, a protest on her lips, Sally firmly held in her hand though it was plain as the dirt at Finn's feet that the little girl wanted to join her brother. "He can watch," Finn allowed, wondering if Miss Morton would call the boy to her.

Miss Lyster went to her side. "Delcie, let Kent enjoy having a man around. You can see them from the window."

"You know I'm nervous about strangers."

35

"I know. Would you feel better if I stayed outside and worked on the garden?"

Miss Morton nodded. "I would. Thank you."

"Then I shall."

Miss Morton tugged Sally back into the house and closed the door firmly. Seconds later, she appeared at the window, Sally's face next to hers.

Miss Lyster grabbed a pair of cotton gloves and a hoe and went to the tiny potato plants.

Finn couldn't help but notice the plants were closer to where the fence was to be built than the rest of the garden. As if she planned to keep a close eye on him.

It might be a relief to Miss Morton to know her friend was nearby, but it made tension grip Finn's neck. He wasn't used to having company. Least of all, a pretty young lady. Or a child, though the latter did not cause the same reaction.

According to the letter Kent would be near the same age as Eddie. And like Kent, he was way too young to be without a mother or father. And much too young to live in the mountains with a man who preferred to be alone.

Finn grabbed the handles of the auger and gave it a mighty twist. One thing he knew for certain. Hard work erased worried, pointless thoughts.

But turning the auger only served to turn his thoughts from one troubling thing to another. Ethel was sending her son to him. He couldn't take care of the boy. He'd have to find someone else to do it. He paused to wipe his brow and glanced at Miss Lyster working in the garden, humming as she hoed. Eighteen years old, she'd said. In his twenty-four years, he'd likely lived two lifetimes to her young years. Yet there was something about her. Something that had brought her west without a man. Was she looking for one? Or like him, running from something? Having heard her laugh, seen her smile, watched her with the children, he couldn't imagine.

She seemed to like the children. Was she anxious to have some of her own?

He shook his head and returned to digging post holes.

He was a cautious man. He did not make quick judgments or decisions.

WORKING in the garden was a peaceful activity for Jenny. To see the plants growing, to think of the fresh vegetables they'd enjoy, to plan gathering and preserving them for the winter and to feel the sun and wind on her face. She found it healing.

She smiled as she thought of her word choice, and yet it was entirely correct. Not that she totally forgot the pain of her past. And she hoped she never would. But the past was behind her and the future looked good.

Finn worked on digging a hole. Kent played nearby, surrounding himself with rocks and twigs. It was pleasant to have someone working nearby.

A wagon drove to the garden and a man helped Finn unload the posts then drove away. Finn grabbed the auger and again set to digging.

Jenny watched.

Finn looked up and their gazes connected. He gave a little nod. She thought she almost saw a smile. He pulled the auger from the hole, grabbed a post and dropped it in then began to tamp the dirt around it.

He could work faster if someone held the post steady so he could use both hands to pack the hole.

She set aside her hoe and went over, grabbed the post. "I'll hold it."

He looked ready to protest then shrugged and bent to shovel in more dirt. When he pounded on the soil, the movement jarred through her arm. It was a good solid sensation and she grinned.

He paused to give her a questioning look.

"I feel like I'm doing something..." She couldn't find the right word for how she felt. "Big," she said, after a hesitation.

He tipped his hat back and wiped his sleeve across his brow. "You'll enjoy the benefit it will provide." He nodded toward the garden. "It looks good."

"Thanks. I enjoy working in the soil. Seeing things grow. It's..." She wondered if he would find her word choice odd. "Healing."

He rested the shovel in the dirt, his powerful hands on the handle, and looked at her so intently that she struggled to not break from his gaze.

"Healing? Someone or something has hurt you?"

His voice had deepened. She wanted to think it was sympathy, understanding, or was it disbelief? Did he think someone as young as she didn't know pain from how others treated her? "I wasn't physically wounded." Tears burned at the back of her eyes and she drew in her bottom lip to keep her emotions at bay.

He pulled his hat lower. "Faithful are the wounds of a friend, the Bible says. But not if they are cruel and mean spirited."

How had he guessed at what happened? Something fluttered in her stomach to have a stranger acknowledge the pain of treachery.

His knuckles were white as he gripped the handle of the shovel. Revealing far more than he likely realized.

She drew in a gasp and then spoke without thinking. "You too have been hurt by someone you counted as friend."

He kept his head down and remained motionless.

A sympathetic connection flowed from her veins. "That's why you're a mountain man."

He scooped up dirt and tipped it against the post then banged on it with enough vigor to threaten the life of the handle. Whack. Whack. Whack.

Jenny waited for one of the pauses between the pounding. "Finn, I'm sorry. I spoke out of turn. I didn't mean to offend you."

He slapped the soil three more times, grabbed the top of the post, and tried to shake it. It remained firmly in place. Then he straightened and looked toward the mountains. "I'm not offended. But I don't like to be reminded of what happened."

"I understand." Though from her limited experience, as a *young thing*, she knew it wasn't as easy to forget as one would hope.

He moved to where he planned to dig the next post hole.

She studied his back for a moment then returned to the rows of potatoes, grabbed her hoe, and whacked out the weeds. Yes, there was something healing about gardening. Chopping away the things she didn't like. Putting an end to weeds stealing from good, useful plants.

The door clattered open. Sally raced out. Straight over to Bill.

Jenny dropped her hoe and rushed after her even as Delcie chased after her, calling for her to stop.

"He won't hurt her," Finn called.

Jenny slowed to a stop and grabbed Delcie's arm. "Bill won't hurt her."

"You're taking his word for it?" Delcie's words carried enough heat to fry eggs.

"Yes, and because I've had personal experience with the mule. He's gentle and friendly."

Delcie shook off Jenny's hand. "I'm not prepared to believe it." But Sally had already reached Bill. The mule lowered his head, his ears tipped forward, and let Sally pet him.

"Listen," Jenny said. Although she couldn't make

out the words, she could hear Sally talking to the mule and then laughing.

Bill nodded his head and whinnied.

"He likes children." Finn stood a few feet behind them.

Delcie continued to Sally's side and gently took her by the hand. "How many times have I told you not to leave the yard without my permission?"

Sally hung her head. "I sowwy." She allowed Delcie to walk her back to the house, her lack of enthusiasm clearly communicated by the way she shuffled her feet and hung her head.

Finn chuckled. Bill snorted and Jenny laughed. "She's full of life, that one. And she lets us know how she's feeling even without words."

"You speak with fondness."

She turned, surprised that Finn sounded as if her fondness was unexpected. "She's a very likeable child. Mind you, I believe all children are likeable."

"Even when they are disobedient or cranky?"

He watched her with a keenness she found unexplainable. "I don't think children are much different than adults. If they are acting badly, there is usually a reason." Remembering Isaac and his father, she added, "Although adults sometimes have evil behind their actions, I don't think children ever do."

"Do you hope to have children of your own some day?"

"That's an odd question from someone I barely know."

He shrugged. "Just curious." He grabbed the auger and returned to digging a hole.

She stared after him. His question had poked at a longing she hadn't known she had. Though the truth was she had pushed it aside, buried it deep when she decided to join the others in the move west. She crossed to where he worked. "I like children, but I don't think I'll ever have my own. So I'm grateful I can help Delcie with Sally and Kent."

He turned the auger for a moment, as if he hadn't heard her then brought his attention to her. "You're young. You have plenty of time to have children."

Why did he watch her so keenly?

"I don't plan to marry." For one second she thought she saw a protest in his eyes. Thought he meant to argue with her.

Instead, he said, "There are lots of children who need someone to love them and care for them." He turned back to digging the hole.

Her jaw dropped open. What an odd thing to say. Why would he probe so deeply on the subject?

With no answer forthcoming and no desire to pressure him for an explanation, she grabbed her hoe and returned to the garden.

Except even slashing at the weeds did not bring an end to curiosity over his words.

Did he know of such a child? Or was he speaking of something else entirely?

4

Finn exerted large amounts of energy into digging holes and setting posts in place. But his efforts did nothing to settle his thoughts. Why had he brought up the subject of children to Miss Lyster? She was a single woman. Surely he could find a married couple who would be glad to take in a seven-year old boy.

Except his solitary life had given him few contacts.

There was the Hooper family. The four men had all recently married. Seemed the family was open to children. He knew a couple of them had little ones though he'd paid little attention to whether they were boys or girls or how many there were. After women had started gathering at the ranch, he'd made a point of avoiding the place.

Besides, he was stuck in Willow Creek until the boy arrived, and he'd offered to build the fence.

Leaving the boy here would be easier than having to make a trip to Coulee Crossing Ranch.

All he had to do was convince the women—Miss Lyster especially—that it was a good idea.

Why Miss Lyster?

He couldn't say though her vow that she would never marry was part of the reason. If she had marriage plans, her future husband might object to her having a child. Especially one not her own.

He paused to look at where he planned to build the fence. He could make the work last a week. That would give him time to assess the situation here more carefully and make his case that Eddie belonged here.

Thoughts skittered through his mind like dry, dusty autumn leaves.

Living alone in the mountains had given him little practice at conversational skills with others. Especially women.

Kent had been called to the house and came out again, carrying containers of vegetable peelings that he took to the enclosed chicken pen at the far corner of the yard to throw to the squawking hens. Rather than return to the house, though Miss Morton watched him through the open door, he sauntered over to where Finn worked.

Kent watched for a moment, rocking on his feet.

Finn knew the boy wanted something and waited to see what it was. Finally, he blurted it out.

"You got young'uns?" Kent finally asked.

The question was so unexpected, the wording so

like what he'd expect from a roving cowboy, that Finn stopped work, pretending it was because he needed to wipe his brow so he could consider the boy.

Kent's eyes, brown and trusting, were wide and full of hope. Or was it longing?

Finn had no way of knowing. "No. I don't."

"How come?"

"Well, for one thing I'm not married." He leaned on the auger to watch the boy, feeling he deserved Finn's undivided attention.

"Neither is Auntie Delcie, but she's got us."

"That's true. But I live up in the mountains. No place for children."

"How come?"

"No school. No church." Even as he said that, he knew the same could be said for Willow Creek. It was the parents' job to teach their children the 3 R's and about the Bible. Most of what he knew of both came from his parents. "Are you learning your lessons?"

"Auntie Delcie is teaching me to read and recite." His sorrowful tone brought a smile to Finn's mouth.

"You'll need to know those things wherever you go. Or whatever you do." Finn glanced to his right. Miss Morton watched from the window and Miss Lyster had stopped hoeing to pick weeds by hand. Were they both listening? Was this a good time to say some of the things he wanted to say? Trouble was, he didn't know what they were.

"You went to school?" Kent seemed to have a hankering to know a great deal about Finn. He could think of no reason not to tell him. Besides, he might be able to throw in a few hints about Eddie and his need for a home such as Kent had.

"Some." No need for the boy to know there was a whole world of reasons why he hadn't attended school very much. He looked toward Miss Lyster. Discovered she was looking at him.

Her unusual green eyes riveted his gaze. He couldn't look away even though his nerves twitched at being under her study. What did she see? A man who avoided people? A man more familiar with silence and aloneness than town and company?

Not the sort of man to raise a child.

Kent sighed, bringing Finn's attention back to him. "Aunt Delcie says she'd like to see a real school in town so me and Sally could go to a real school. 'Course Sally is too little right now but Auntie Delcie says maybe by the time Sally is big enough there'll be a school. In the meantime, Auntie will teach me." He sighed again, the idea of school weighing him down.

"If there is a school that means there will be other children." Finn hoped to make Kent understand there were benefits to school apart from an education. "I remember how much fun it was to play with the others."

"What didcha play?"

"Ball, of course, but other games. Pom Pom Pull away, Simon says, Auntie I Over. Lots of them. In the winter, we played checkers, Snakes and Ladders. School was fun."

"Can you show me how to play those games?"

"Most of them take several people. That's why school is fun." Finn turned the auger again and pulled the dirt from the hole.

"There are games you can play without going to school."

Miss Lyster's voice so near at hand sent a shock through Finn's arms. How had he been so distracted he hadn't noticed her approach? One day in town and he was growing careless. A mistake like that in the woods might cost him his life.

He slowly straightened and brought his attention to her as she talked to Kent.

"Like what?" Kent asked. "Can you show me?"

"Sure. There's all sorts of tag games. I'll be It. I'll tag someone. Like this." She tapped Kent then darted away. "Now you're It. Catch someone." She tipped her head toward Finn.

Finn blinked. He shook his head. Surely, she didn't mean...

Kent stared at her, then shifted his gaze to Finn. He grinned as he realized what he was supposed to do and jumped forward to touch Finn.

"You're It." His voice full of glee, he raced away.

Finn stood stock still, his thoughts frozen. So that's how it was to be. He slowly set the auger in the hole. Felt Kent and Miss Lyster waiting. The latter took a step forward. "You have to catch someone."

"Uh huh." He adjusted his hat, wiped his hands on his thighs, and sighed loudly, as if the game was too childish for the likes of him. Then with one leap he reached Kent, grabbed him about the waist, and swung him around. "Now who's it?"

Kent squealed. "You? Me?" He giggled so hard he couldn't talk.

Finn shook him again for good measure than set him on the ground. Kent clung to Finn's hands.

"I like that game."

Finn tipped his head back. He had too. Miss Lyster came closer, her eyes was warm as the morning sun.

"Aunt Jenny, that was fun."

She nodded. "I see that."

"Kent, come here," Miss Morton called.

"Aww." But the boy obeyed.

Finn watched him leave, keeping his attention on the boy to avoid Miss Lyster's continued study of him.

"Thank you for playing with him." Her gentle voice drew his gaze to her.

"I haven't played for a long time." He heard the regret and sadness in his tone but hoped she didn't.

"Right. Because you are so old."

He nodded. "Been old a long time."

"You aren't talking about years, are you?"

"No, I suppose not." He would have returned to his work, but she stood between him and the hole he'd been digging. So he waited.

"You must have been a child at one time."

"A long while ago. And for a short time."

She contemplated his words. "Your childhood was short? Why?"

He hadn't talked about himself in so long, he couldn't remember how. But what better way to make it understood that he couldn't take a child and raise him. The words came slowly, haltingly. "I was orphaned when I was eight. That ended my childhood."

She drew in a sharp breath. "Finn, I'm sorry." A beat of silence. "What happened to your parents?"

"They died in a wagon accident." He had never known the full details and it no longer mattered.

"What became of you?"

"A family took me in. The Moores. They often took in orphaned children and taught them to work."

She waited.

He said nothing, letting the words sink in.

"Work? That's it?"

"Working is what made the Moores keep me and others like me." He shrugged. "What else can an orphaned child expect?"

She drew herself up tall. Her eyes flashed. "First of all, love and affection. Also, at least a basic education and time to be a child."

It was the answer he hoped for.

"I agree. But not everyone sees it that way. I'm glad to see orphaned children receive it here."

Her gaze went to the house from where came the sound of children laughing. "They certainly do."

He tried to find a way to suggest another child would be a nice addition. Especially a boy. But the words refused to come.

"I must help with supper." She hurried away and he returned to digging holes.

Bill sauntered over to Finn's side and nudged him on the shoulder as if to commiserate with Finn's frustration at not knowing how to ask Miss Lyster if she'd take the boy.

Bill butted his head into Finn's back.

Seems the mule wasn't sympathetic at all. He was disappointed in Finn's failure to communicate with a pretty woman.

Bill never had that problem. Women liked him. And he liked them.

Poor animal, stuck with Finn.

Poor Eddie, if he too ended up stuck with Finn.

Somehow Finn had to get his words together to speak to Miss Lyster about the boy.

* * *

As JENNY SLICED bread for the evening meal, her gaze went often to the window through which she could see Finn working. The man had lost his family at such a young age. And been made to work. She guessed that meant no school, no family life. The end of his childhood.

No wonder Finn was so...distant? Reserved? Cautious?

Had his loss and subsequent way of life driven him to the mountains where he had no one to please but himself?

"I hope we don't have cause to regret allowing him to stay." Delcie's words already held a whole lot of regret. She mashed the potatoes with more vigor than they required.

"He was orphaned at eight." Jenny thought the knowledge might spark a bit of compassion in Delcie.

Laura and Hilda both murmured a sound of sympathy. Likely they all thought of Kent and Sally.

Delcie's hands grew still and her gaze riveted to the scene beyond the river. "Was he taken in by a family or sent to an orphanage?" A shudder crossed her shoulders at the thought of how orphaned children were often treated.

"A family took him in and, in his words, taught him to work."

Delcie turned her gaze to Jenny. "You watch that man. Children raised without love often turn into conscienceless people." Her eyes were hard as ice. "I don't want the children around him."

Sally and Kent had been sent to straighten the dining room but returned in time to overhear Delcie's comment.

"You talking about me and Mr. Johnson?" Kent's voice shook with his emotion. "He's a nice man. He has a nice mule. I like him." He crossed his arms and stuck out his chin.

Sally looked at her brother and then imitated his stance. "I do's too."

Jenny turned away to hide her smile.

"He played with me," Kent persisted.

"I'll play with you." Delcie smiled. She left the potato masher in the pot, wiped her hands on her apron, and moved toward the children, reaching out her arms to hug them.

Kent backed away and Sally followed his example.

"You can't swing me in the air," he said. "'Sides. I need to see how a man works."

"Me, too," Sally echoed.

Jenny exchanged amused glances with Hilda and Laura. How would Delcie answer that?

"He's here to do a job," she said. "Not to play with children. You two stay out of his way." She gave the potatoes two more jabs as if to announce the discussion was over.

Kent took Sally's hand and returned to the dining room, glancing back to give Delcie a look rife with anger.

Hilda broke the awkward silence that followed their departure. "Delcie, you can't keep them shut up indoors so you can be in control of who they speak to." Her accent deepened, revealing how little she liked this sort of upset.

"I can keep them inside until that man leaves."

"Is that fair?"

"It's fair to me."

Hilda went to Delcie and patted her on her shoulder. "You moved halfvay across the country so they could be safe and free to be children. Are you going to take that avay because of your own suspicions?"

Delcie kept her attention on the window. Her expression remained hard, unrelenting.

"I thought you would be sympathetic to him because of him being an orphan." Jenny wondered at her friend's lack of compassion. "Maybe God has brought him into our midst so we can show him that family doesn't have to be father, mother, and children. Look at us. We are family even though we aren't bound by a marriage contract or have children born to us."

Delcie spun around to face Jenny. "Are you suggesting that we welcome him into our family?" Her mouth twisted. Her eyes darkened.

Jenny's smile was half grimace. "That isn't what I said. But—" How was she to explain this feeling she had? That he could benefit from being around them even as they would benefit with the construction of a fence? "It wouldn't hurt to make him a little welcome, would it?"

Delcie's mouth tightened. Her eyes narrowed. Her footsteps were hurried and her heels hard on the floor as she moved to glance out at the dining room. "Our first customers have arrived." She rushed from the room to take the order though the choice was simple —supper was ready, take it or leave it.

She must have said something to the children as they scuffled into the kitchen. "Aunt Delcie says we should help," Kent said with as much enthusiasm as if he'd been sent to muck out a barn.

Jenny smiled. He'd likely prefer that task, especially

if Finn was in the barn. Her gaze went to the window. Finn tamped another post into place. How long would it take for him to build a fence? Could she do something while he was there to show him friendship? Something besides work. A child, and yes, a man, was worth more than that.

Just like a pretty woman, whose eyes seemed to invite men to stare, was worth more than admiration for her looks. Admiration and rejection. But not acceptance and value as a whole person.

Delcie returned and ordered three meals. Jenny helped prepare the dishes. And then a couple dozen others entered, and she was kept busy. Their business was doing better than expected. She didn't know where so many people came from, and she wasn't about to complain.

But she wasn't too busy to think and plan. There had to be a way to make Finn feel welcome besides feeding him. A way that would make him understand that it wasn't just his work that mattered. Perhaps it was silly on her part, but it seemed she had to prove it to him as a means of erasing the sting of the words spoken by Isaac and his father. *Too pretty to make a good wife.* She needed to prove those words untrue, and what better way than helping Finn?

By the time all the guests had been served and eaten their meal and she began to gather up dirty dishes and carry out dessert, she had come up with a plan that she meant to start carrying out immediately.

inn deepened the hole he was digging. He kept his back to the house, but he couldn't shut out the sounds of a number of people coming in for a meal. Was it the same group as earlier? But he'd heard the mule train leaving even before he started to build the fence. He was familiar with the area and knew there weren't that many people living nearby.

Curious, he shifted so he could see those entering the establishment. To his surprise, they weren't all men. There were women and children. Families. That didn't make sense.

Two young fellas, grown to the size of a man but still wet behind the ears, wandered to the back of the lot. They saw Bill and one said he'd never seen a spotted donkey before.

Mule, Finn silently corrected.

The other laughed and said, "Looks like someone spilled their breakfast on him."

Laughing, they moved closer.

Bill's ears went back.

Finn dropped the auger and leaped forward. "Boys, better keep your distance. He's been known to be bad tempered."

The pair jerked around, surprised at Finn's sudden appearance.

"Where did you come from?" one asked.

Finn jerked his thumb over his shoulder to indicate where he'd been working. "I might ask you the same thing."

"We're with a wagon train camped down by the creek. On our way to Fort Edmonton."

That would explain all those entering the cafe. "Big train?"

"Twenty families."

Families? Just what he needed for Eddie. "You plan on being here long?"

"Only long enough to make some repairs."

Could Finn hope the repairs would last until Eddie arrived? "I might mosey along and say howdy."

"You do that." The speaker nudged his companion. "Come on. Let's go see if the food is as good as they say it is. And the gals are as pretty." The pair laughed and strode away.

At the idea of the two of them ogling the ladies, Finn had half a mind to tell Bill to kick them both. Instead, he returned to digging holes and planting posts. He'd work until dark. Just as he'd been taught by Mr. Moore.

"Come in for supper."

Miss Lyster's voice so near at hand made him jump. He'd been trying *not* to think of her...and the others.

"I'll work until dark." It's what he was used to.

"No need."

"It's what I do." He turned the auger around.

She eased past him so she could look in his face. "There is more to life than work."

Despite having learned to keep his opinions to himself, he snorted. "Yeah. There are the mountains. Where a man answers to no one but himself and nature."

"And God?"

He stopped twisting the hands of the auger and met her look. Those green eyes gave him the same jolt as the first time he saw them. Paler toward the center with a darker rim. "You have unusual eyes." What happened to learning to keep his opinions to himself? He lowered his gaze. "I'm sorry. That was inappropriate. Pretend I didn't say it." He rushed on. "When I say nature, I include God. A man can't live up there and not be aware of God's presence."

"'In His hand are the deep places of the earth: the strength of the hills is His also.' That's from Psalm 95. And apology accepted. You aren't the first person to comment on my eyes."

His head came up as she spoke the words from the

Bible, so he was able to see the way her lips narrowed as she mentioned her eyes. He regretted that he'd said something that made her look so anxious but didn't know what to do but let it go. The less he said, the better off he was. A lesson that was deeply ingrained in his mind. Instead, he addressed the other part of what she said.

"You speak from memory. Brings to mind the Hooper family. Blaze Hooper gave me a Bible to read and told me how his parents, especially his mother, taught them to memorize verses." Finn's reading skills were limited but with no one to scold or mock, he took his time and found his ability improving to the point he enjoyed reading the scriptures. "Blaze said I should try it. I think he figured it would give me something to do while I was all by myself." His grin was crooked as he remembered Blaze's words. Blaze simply couldn't imagine a man being happy alone. "I've always had my brothers and my sister," he'd said. "I admit, they're sometimes annoying, but at least I'm never wanting for someone to talk to."

"I know of the Hoopers. You must be acquainted with Audrey, though she's now Mrs. Holmen. She's a good friend of Hilda's...Mrs. Meyers. It was at her suggestion that Hilda decided to start this business. Audrey came to visit us shortly after we arrived. She is so happy to be mama to three little ones."

"I've met the woman." When he visited the Hoopers' ranch, the brothers had insisted he join them indoors for coffee and cookies. Mention of the three children brought Finn's mind back to his need to find a home for Eddie. If he ate now, he could slip away and visit the wagon train before dark. Assess the possibilities.

"I do believe I will stop now and enjoy that food. The aroma has been making my mouth water the last hour." He gathered up the tools and carried them to the shed beside the chicken house.

She followed him, leaning against the doorjamb of the shed while he stored the tools. "I'm grateful you suggested building a fence. Gives me hope I can grow all the plants I have planned."

He closed the door and she straightened and fell into step with him as they crossed the yard, skirting the planted garden.

She paused at the door and bent to lift the leaves of a wilted plant. "I guess it's unrealistic to expect all the plants I dig up to survive. But I hate losing any of them." She straightened and dusted her hands together. "Come in."

He followed her inside and stood waiting with his hat in his hands. Did he go through to the dining room or sit at the cupboard? After all, he wasn't a paying guest. He was working for his meal. By his own choice, not because someone made him. But did that make any difference in the eyes of others?

She grabbed a plate and filled it to overflowing and handed it to him. He waited for her to indicate what he should do. She picked up a second one, filled it about half as much.

The other ladies were busy with washing dishes and cleaning the kitchen, but he was aware of them watching every move.

Miss Morton kept a firm hand on Kent's shoulder, pinning him in place. Kent was not pleased about it.

"I want to sit with Finn while he eats." The boy pleaded with his aunt. "I'm going to ask him about being a mountain man. Could be that's what I'm going to be."

"You are staying right here, young man. As soon as the dishes are done, you are going to have a reading lesson."

Kent's mouth drew back, and his eyes narrowed.

"Even a mountain man needs to be able to read and write and cipher," Finn said in a soft voice that he hoped invited argument from no one.

Kent sighed. "I guess so."

Miss Lyster watched the exchange then turned to Finn. "Come on." She went to the dining room.

He followed as far as the doorway. The room was now empty. She sat at a table near the display case and waved toward the chair across from her.

She expected him to sit and eat with her? To refuse would be rude. To accept would be…

He didn't know. He only knew it didn't feel right. But he crossed the floor and sat where she'd indicated.

She smiled. "Would you like to say grace?" She bowed her head.

Him say grace? In front of her? He'd never prayed aloud before anyone except Bill and God. Maybe if he imagined her to be Bill... But although he tried, he couldn't replace her pretty face with Bill's long nose and ears. He gulped loudly.

Lord, help me not die of embarrassment. "Let us come before His presence with thanksgiving. Amen." He made it through without choking and kept his attention on his plate when he opened his eyes. She must think him an idiot.

"Finn, did you know that's part of the same Psalm I quoted earlier?"

"It is?" He had no idea where the words had come from. Maybe he retained more of what he read than he knew.

"And a lovely way to say grace."

He stared at her. But she didn't look like she was teasing or mocking. She smiled gently, making light sparkle in her eyes. Or was that the sun's rays slanting through the west window? Not knowing what to think or do, he turned his attention to the food, which was delicious. "Good food," he said.

"Thanks. We all help, but it's mostly Hilda's doing. Delcie and I like to make desserts. Laura is the best pie maker of us all."

"Sounds like a nice arrangement."

"It's ideal for us. But tell me about yourself. Do you have family?"

"I'm the only one left of my family."

"That is truly sad. To be so alone."

"Well, I'm not all alone. I have Bill."

Her laughter rang out, not loud, but so musical he wondered if the birds outside had stopped to listen.

She sobered and her eyes held his. He realized he was staring. Knew he had to stop but couldn't.

"I don't believe Bill has much to say," she said.

"Oh, don't be fooled. Bill is plenty opinionated. But he is a mule of few words."

She grinned. "You must get lonely up on your mountain."

"Well, it's not my mountain. It's just where I live."

"How long were you with the Moores?"

"Six years."

She had cleaned her plate and tipped her head from side to side as she studied him. "What happened to you at fourteen?"

"A new boy took my place, so I was on my own."

She sat back, her eyes wide. "Homeless? What did you do?"

"I worked. I found work around town for a couple of years then decided it was time to move on."

"Why would you stay around? I'd expect you to head off to a life of excitement."

He couldn't imagine why she would say such a thing unless she thought living on the mountainside was a yearning for adventure. "It was the only home I knew, even if I wasn't welcome to visit."

"You weren't even allowed to visit? That seems a little cruel."

He looked at the sun blaring through the window. "Could be because of their daughter."

"Their daughter? Why? What happened?"

He pushed to his feet. "I have to go. I've got to look after Bill."

"What about dessert?"

"Don't have time. Thanks for the meal." He hurried from the room and into the warm spring air. Had he really said something about Ethel? Admitted the very thing he'd spent years trying to forget? The subject he'd vowed he would never mention. The pain and disappointment that had driven him into the mountains. The last thing he wanted was to refresh those memories. And the words she had uttered that last time.

He called Bill. He'd go to his campsite and forget this whole unfortunate day.

* * *

JENNY STARED at the closed door through which Finn had so suddenly disappeared. Why would he mention the daughter and then rush away as if it was something he didn't want to talk about? It didn't make sense. But it seemed the girl was responsible for him being driven from the home. Was it also responsible for him hiding in the mountains? What had happened? Had he done something inappropriate? She shook her head. Although she knew little of him, it seemed to her that he was so concerned with doing the right thing, not crossing any boundaries, not taking anything for granted, that he would not be guilty of something evil. Then what could it be? Was he responsible for an accident that left her crippled? Or worse? That would be horrible. Whatever happened, he must live with constant regret and hurt.

Hilda appeared at the kitchen doorway. "He left in a hurry. Vas it something you said?"

"I don't think so." It was something he'd said. "Said he had to take care of his mule."

His pace hurried, Finn passed before the front windows, Bill at his heels. He glanced neither to the right nor the left.

Very strange behavior.

She carried the dishes to the kitchen and washed them. Delcie had taken the children to the bedroom she shared with them and could be heard reading to them. How fortunate the children were to have someone as devoted and loving as Delcie.

"Where's Laura?" Jenny asked Hilda.

"She's gone outside to read. You know how she loves this time of day."

"Is there anything that needs doing?"

"I don't think so. Everything is ready for the morning. Vhy don't you go enjoy the evening like the rest of us are?"

Knowing Hilda liked to have the kitchen to herself once the work was done, Jenny left through the back door. Laura sat in the shade of the house, reading. The fence posts Finn had placed stood alone and stark.

Like the man who had placed them there?

She left Laura to her solitude and stepped from the

yard. She walked along the dusty street. Like Hilda said, it was nice to enjoy the evening once the work was done. Usually she found the time restful, but her thoughts today were troubled.

Finn had a secret, and it behooved her to find out what it was even though she'd already decided it couldn't be anything bad. But she had to make sure. For the sake of the children and the others, she told herself, ignoring her own burning curiosity.

From down by the creek that had given Willow Creek its name, there came the sounds of the newest visitors. The mooing of cattle, the rattle of wagons and pots and pans, the murmur of voices with the occasional burst of laughter. She might as well go there and greet the people from the wagon train.

She soon reached the wagons and spoke to the circle of women. Some had come to the diner for supper but there were many who hadn't. She glanced around, glimpsed Finn talking to a group of men beyond the wagons. He seemed keenly interested in the conversation. Perhaps she'd get a chance to ask him what happened with the Moore's daughter.

The women invited her to sit and visit and plied her with questions about the area. She learned some were seasoned farmers and pioneers. Others were city people who faced the challenges of the future with much courage.

One young mother confessed she'd never before milked a cow and now her husband expected her to.

"He's been kind enough to teach me, but there is so much to learn."

"You'll do just fine," Jenny said. "There isn't anything you can't learn to do if you have the desire."

"Well, I'm stubborn, if that counts."

The women all laughed.

A little later, Jenny looked toward where Finn had been. The group of men had disbanded, and she didn't see him. It seemed she wouldn't get a chance to talk to him tonight. Ah well. There was always tomorrow.

She said good-bye and left the circle of women. She hadn't realized that dusk had fallen while she was visiting. It was almost dark out. She hurried along the path back to town.

Rustling grass sent tremors up her spine to the top of her head. She should have been more aware of the time. She increased her pace. Footsteps thudded behind her. It could be someone going about his own business.

Or it could be someone meaning her harm.

Her hands grew clammy as she hurried along.

Lamps burned in the windows of the homes ahead. A golden glow of hope. She would soon reach the diner and her friends. And safety.

A man appeared at her right. Another at her left. Her chest tightened impossibly at their sudden appearance, making each breath ache in and out.

"Yer too purty to be out alone," one said.

She didn't respond to the comment. *Too pretty*. How she hated those words. Especially when she'd just proven she wasn't very smart, or she wouldn't be in this situation.

"Maybe she's deaf," the second man said.

She slowed, hoping they would continue on without her.

They didn't.

Instead they stopped and blocked her path.

The faint moonlight allowed her a glimpse of their faces. She was sure the pair had been at the diner earlier. Callow youth. Feeling the freedom and challenges of the trail.

Youth or not, they were dangerous. Her stomach churned.

Forcing her voice to be firm she said, "Please let me pass." She took a step forward, but they widened their stances and crossed their arms, letting her know they didn't intend to let her by. The trembling that had claimed her innards caught at her arms. She stiffened. She would not let them know how frightened she was.

"What's your rush?"

"My friends will be looking for me."

"The more the merrier." Both boys chortled.

Jenny's skin crawled. If there was there anything more dangerous than a boy in a man's body, it was two of them. She flinched at the snap of a nearby twig. Was another youth about to join them? She had to get away. She rushed forward, hoping to break through between them.

Instead, they caught her and pinned her arms to

her sides. One of them covered her mouth with his hand.

She kicked and twisted and tried to bite the hand. She squirmed, trying to get away, but two of them holding her made it impossible.

Oh Lord, help me.

6

inn had taken care of Bill and left him at his campsite with instructions to stay put. He'd pushed aside his regret at having mentioned Ethel and reminded himself of the need to find a family for Eddie. He'd joined the men around the wagon train and talked to several. There didn't seem to be a subtle way of asking if Eddie would be welcome, so he'd been blunt. "Anyone wanting to take in an orphan boy?" Though to be accurate, he didn't know if Eddie was not an orphan yet.

Several of the men had shaken their heads and said they couldn't afford to feed another mouth.

"Is he big enough to work?" one man asked.

"He's seven." Finn had bristled at the question. Not that he expected anything else. Except he did. The boy should have affection and an education. Book learning, not just learning from the school of hard knocks.

"That's big enough. I might be interested. Could use someone to herd the cows on the trail."

Finn had seen a number of the men shuffle their feet and look uncomfortable. "I'll give it some thought." It was what he wanted, wasn't it? A family to take the boy. Except it wasn't. He couldn't think of putting any child with a man who cared only how much work he could get out of a youngster. Could be Eddie was smallish. But even if he was big a boy, he needed more than work.

Finn knew there was something about that thought that was contrary to what he believed for himself, but he wasn't a man to probe too deeply into his own feelings. Seemed to him that only brought unrest and unhappiness.

He'd turned away at the sound of a familiar laugh and saw Miss Lyster visiting with a group of ladies. He'd backed into the shadows and watched. She was like a butterfly amongst a bunch of moths.

She rose, spoke to the ladies, then headed down the darkening path toward town.

He watched her until she was out of sight then took a step, intending to return to his camp. A movement out of the corner of his eyes stopped him. Two young fellas left the campfire and sauntered away. He recognized them as the two who had called Bill a donkey. They could be going about their own business, but he would wait and make sure they didn't have mischief up their sleeves. They seemed the sort who might.

Sure enough, they headed down the same trail Miss Lyster had taken. Might be innocent enough, but Finn meant to make sure. He eased around the trees, sticking to the shadows and followed, silent as the pail moonlight.

Despite his care, a twig snapped beneath his feet. Not that anyone but him noticed. He was still several yards behind when the pair joined Miss Lyster than grabbed her. She struggled. He could only imagine how terrified she must be.

Fury burned along his veins and he leaped forward, grabbing the two by the back of their shirts and yanking them off her. Surprised, they scrambled to retain their footing.

One stammered, "We weren't doing nothin'."

"Let me go." The other swung his fist and landed a blow to Finn's belly, driving the air from him in a whoosh.

He retained his hold and shook the pair. "I don't think the wagon master would approve of what you're doing." He'd spoken to the man and taken him to be someone who ran things according to rules. He'd ask him to keep an eye on this pair.

The first boy got his feet under him. "Sir, please let me go. I won't bother her again. I promise."

"Don't bother anyone, hear? It's the sign of a small man to pick on someone weaker." Finn didn't release him but twisted his fist into the fabric of the other young man's shirt. "And you. What do you have to say?"

"I'm sorry. Now let me go." The tone was anything but repentant.

Finn released the first boy and grabbed the other to shake him hard. He pressed his face close. "I'll be watching you. If you so much as look at Miss Lyster I'll deal with you, and it won't be pretty. Now git." He pushed the boy away. The young man scrambled for his footing and then the pair hurried back down the trail.

Finn turned his attention to Miss Lyster, who had backed away until the trees stopped her.

"You're safe now." He kept his distance from her, not wanting to frighten her further.

Her breathing was ragged, catching, as if she held back sobs.

"I'll walk you the rest of the way home." He waited but she didn't move. "Miss Lyster, you are safe now."

She shuddered so hard the tree she leaned on quaked. She was pale, but it might have only been the weak moonlight that made her appear so. Still, he worried she might pass out.

He edged closer, cautiously, watching for any sign of his approach alarming her.

She sank to the ground and buried her face in her palms.

He hunkered down close by, prepared to let her have all the time she needed to collect herself.

"I shouldn't have been here. I should have been aware of how late it was getting. I wasn't careful enough. Mr. Stanley was right. I'm nothing but a pretty face. I don't have any sense. Nice to look at but not good for anything else." Her words were muffled by her hands and fractured by her shaking voice, but he knew he'd heard her correctly.

"It's not a weakness to be pretty."

"No, it's a curse. Makes men think they can take advantage of me." Bitterness dripped from every word, burning a trail through Finn's heart and mind.

Seemed she'd been subject to unwelcome attention before. He didn't want to think exactly what those actions might have been. All that mattered right now was getting her calmed down and back home to safety. "I'm sorry you've been treated poorly. You don't deserve that. Ever."

She remained with her face to her palms, her breath jerking in and out.

He had to think of something more to calm her down. "You're pretty. That's for sure. Your eyes are unusually beautiful." His throat tightened at how familiar he was being. The very thing she feared. He went on, hoping he could make her understand he meant her no harm, only good. "But you're more than that. You are a hard worker. You help run the diner. And you have a big garden with amazing plans to make it not just useful but beautiful too. I'd say that was a combination much like yourself." He had not spoken so many words to a woman all at once in years. He hoped he hadn't offended her. Maybe made things worse.

Her breathing slowed. She sucked in a deep breath

and then straightened. "Useful and beautiful. I like that. That is my aim."

He waited for her to indicate if she was ready to continue homeward.

She sighed and leaned her head back. "Too bad Mr. Stanley and his son couldn't see that possibility."

It was the second time he'd heard that name, and already he didn't like it. "What did this Mr. Stanley do?"

She stiffened then she got to her feet. "I'm going home."

He scrambled up beside her. "I'll walk you back."

"Thank you. I appreciate that."

They walked along the pathway until they reached the street. In a few minutes they would be back at the diner. She'd be relieved to be with her friends and away from men. Though he hoped she saw him differently than that pair who had stopped her. Or Mr. Stanley, whoever he was and whatever he'd done.

They reached the yard and he stopped. She took two steps then turned. "Finn, thank you for rescuing me and making me feel better." Then she hurried across the yard and into the house.

He watched until the door closed firmly behind her. "You're welcome," he whispered, and wondered at the feeling pressing at the encasement of his heart. Was it sympathy, regret, or a desire to make Miss Lyster understand that she was more than a beautiful woman?

Not that it was up to him to prove it to her. He was

only here to do a job while he waited for Eddie to arrive. His search for a family from the wagon train had not been productive but he could go back to his original plan. In fact, what better way to make Miss Lyster realize her value than to entrust her with the care of a child?

Finn skirted around the wagon train and returned to his camp.

Bill trotted forward to greet him.

"Missed me, didcha?"

The mule rumbled his lips and pressed his head to Finn's shoulder. "Had things to do," Finn said as he unpacked his bedroll and tossed it on the ground near some trees.

Bill edged in between Finn and the bedroll.

"Look, I don't feel like talking. I'm going to bed." He pulled off his boots and put them by his resting spot where he could quickly don them. He slipped his vest off and hung it over a branch then lay down.

Bill snuffled and snorted then moseyed away a few feet and grabbed a mouthful of grass. His way of saying he didn't care for Finn's company at the moment.

Finn closed his eyes and willed sleep to come. But his thoughts circled like angry hornets. Ethel. Eddie. Miss Lyster. Round and round the names raced, leaving him dizzy and confused.

Why had he mentioned Ethel? It wasn't like he'd thought of her much lately. But getting a letter from her made it impossible to forget her. Why would she ask him to take Eddie? Especially after her last dismissive words. She'd made it clear that he didn't meet with her approval. Why would he be approved as a guardian for a child? Not that he could take the boy. He'd find other arrangements and return to his cabin. The sooner the better. Perhaps he'd ask Burnsie to make sure the boy got to a suitable place.

But he couldn't leave without finishing the job he'd taken on for Miss Lyster. Jenny. He liked that name. Enough of that. He had no room in his life for anyone. Child or woman.

He'd stay until the job was completed and, despite wishing he didn't feel responsible, he'd stay and make sure Eddie got a good home. That brought him full circle back to Miss Lyster. She seemed a good person. Her friends would help her raise the boy. All he had to do was find a way to bring up the topic.

* * *

JENNY STEPPED into the kitchen and gulped. Her three friends stood in the middle of the floor, worried expressions filling their faces.

"Vat happened to you?" Hilda asked, her accent heavy, indicating her emotional state. "Ve vas so vorried."

Laura sprang forward and rubbed her hand along Jenny's arm. "Are you all right? Did something happen?"

Delcie's mouth worked. "I was afraid someone had

taken you." After the children had been snatched back in Broadstone, Manitoba before they left, Delcie lived in fear it would happen to them again. Or to one of her friends.

Jenny smiled, hoping it was steady and looked genuine. "I'm sorry to cause you all worry. I went to visit the ladies down at the creek and time got away on me."

"You're sure that's all?" Delcie would struggle to lose her suspicions that something horrible had happened to Jenny. And Jenny didn't want to add to Delcie's worry.

"You're shaking. You're upset about something. What happened?" Laura's gentle voice ended Jenny's fragile hold on her self-control.

"Two young men accosted me." She told what had happened. Telling it made the situation fresh and frightening and she struggled not to reveal how much it had alarmed her. "Thankfully, Finn came along when he did." He'd been so understanding. Too bad she had let his kindness make her mention the Stanleys.

As she talked, her friends led her to a chair and had her sit then gathered around her, comforting and soothing.

"Ve must thank him," Hilda said.

Laura rubbed Jenny's arm. "It's nice to know there might be a decent man to be found."

Delcie shook her head. "We aren't so foolish as to trust him simply because he did the right thing in this situation, though I am grateful he was there when you needed him." She smiled but Jenny could see the fear and caution lingering in her eyes.

Jenny looked around at her friends. "I'm sorry I caused you to worry, but I'm fine. Are the children asleep?"

Delcie gave a trembling smile. "It took a bit to settle them. Kent kept talking about your mountain man."

"He's not mine! Why would you say such a thing?" Her cheeks burned. If they knew the kind words he'd spoken they would be doubly convinced of that notion.

Hilda chuckled. "Vell, it is you who vanted him to build the fence and you who spent all afternoon out there with him. Need I mention you vaited until he came in to eat to have your supper vhich, I might point out, you ate vith him?"

"I'm only trying to be friendly. I feel sorry for the man. He lives a solitary life and seems so...so..." How could she describe this feeling she had? "Wounded." That made her appear to know more about him than she did. "Alone, I guess is what I mean."

Laura squeezed Jenny's arm. "Of course you feel sorry for him. That's understandable. And now you are grateful to him, as we all are."

Jenny didn't bother trying to explain that she didn't feel sorry for him. How could she when she didn't understand what she felt?

"Just be careful," Delcie said. "We all know that you can't trust what you see on the surface."

"Of course I'll be careful."

Hilda lifted a hand. "Girls, I think ve're all relieved that Jenny is all right though she did have us vorried a bit. And I'm sure she vill be cautious. She has as much reason as any of us to be so. Now let's turn in. Morning comes early. Good night." She went to the room she shared with Laura and Jenny where they each had a narrow cot. Delcie retired to the room she shared with the children.

Jenny prepared for bed and crawled between the covers. "Good night," she whispered, and the others replied softly.

By rights, Jenny should have fallen asleep immediately. After all, they rose early to bake bread and start the day's food. Normally, bread was their biggest seller, but the last couple of days they had scrambled to keep up with the meals. On top of rising early and working in the hot kitchen, she had spent several hours working in the garden. Her body was weary and needed rest, but her mind had things to sort out before it would let her sleep.

Why had she blurted out Mr. Stanley's name? Of course, Finn wanted to know who he was and what he'd done. Not that she meant to tell him. That was a part of her life she wanted to forget.

Thank you, God, for sending Finn along when I needed him.

She didn't like to think what those youths would

have done. She eased to her side and stared at the wall. She needed something to calm her thoughts. If not for the fact she would have disturbed the others, she would have lit the lamp and read her Bible.

A smile curved her mouth as she remembered Finn quoting a Bible verse as a grace. And from the same Psalm she had quoted earlier. It was like a sign.

A snort started in the top of her mouth, but she remembered in time that she shared the room with two others and quelled the sound. What sort of sign did she think it was? She wasn't foolish enough to think it meant they shared something special. Yes, she felt gratitude to him for rescuing her. And she still desired to make him understand they welcomed him for more than the work he said he'd do. Poor little orphan boy. Too bad someone like Delcie hadn't rescued him and shown him love. *Love covereth all sins.*

Where had those words come from? Was it a verse from the Bible? Was she like Finn and remembering verses without knowing she was?

What did it mean? Surely not that she was to love him like a man and woman. Her cheeks burned to think of it. But he said she was beautiful as well as useful. The words settled into her heart with all the intention of taking up permanent roost. They went a long way toward erasing the Stanleys' words.

Not that she would ever forget them nor how they made her feel.

Love came in many forms. Could she show Finn the kind of love a friend had for a friend? In a sense, hadn't that been her goal from the first? To make him feel welcome and see that he didn't have to work to be of value?

She smiled as she realized that what they each needed seemed to be the opposite of what the other needed. He needed to think less of work, and she needed to feel that her work was acknowledged. What a strange situation.

Sleep claimed her. Hilda's alarm wakened them before dawn and they scurried to get bread in pans, biscuits rolled and ready to bake, and a batch of cookies mixed up. As soon as that was done, Jenny hurried out to get the eggs. It was impossible to guess how many people would show up for breakfast. Usually no more than half a dozen. But they had to be prepared to cook for more because of the wagon train.

The solid fence posts caught her attention, reminding her of Finn. Not that she'd forgotten. Anymore than she'd forgotten her fright at how those two young men had treated her. As she stared at the posts, she made up her mind.

Finn had said something about the Moore's daughter that caused her to think it had left him hurting and alone. She meant to discover what it was in the hopes of helping him.

After all, he'd rescued her. Maybe by ferreting out the truth, she could rescue him right back.

ith the sounds of those at the wagon train intruding on his quiet, Finn ate a cold breakfast at his camp even though he knew he could enjoy a hot meal at the diner. He needed time to sort his thoughts and prepare himself. But after he'd rolled up his bedroll, cleaned up his campsite, and taken Bill to the creek for water, he didn't feel any more ready than when he first opened his eyes.

"You coming or staying here?" he asked his mule, knowing the answer.

Bill trotted at his heels as they made their way to the diner. He went in at the back and directly to the shed to get the tools he needed and set to work digging the next hole.

He kept his back to the kitchen but heard the door open and Kent call, "Hello. You came back. I knew you would."

Finn stopped work to greet the boy. "I have to finish the job I took on."

"I could help."

Finn saw Miss Morton rush from the window. Knew she'd appear at the door in a matter of seconds. "I don't think your aunt would approve."

"Kent." The call was firm.

Kent sighed. "I have to go." He brightened. "But I'll come back."

"You get your aunt's permission first."

"I will." He raced toward the house. Moments later he came out with a pail, went to the chicken yard, and tossed out the contents. The hens ran after it with much clucking and jostling for position.

Finn grinned. Chickens could be so aggressive when it came to food.

Several times, the boy ran in and out of the house on errands. He carried in several armloads of wood. He brought out dishwater and carefully watered the wilted plants with Miss Lyster supervising.

When he returned to the house, Miss Lyster crossed to where Finn worked.

Shouldn't he have his words all corralled and ready to speak? But instead he had a mind full of nothing.

"Kent is eager to do his chores. Delcie gave him a long list of things to do and said he could help you when he was done." She chuckled. "I think she hoped the chores would keep him busy all morning. I've never seen him move so fast."

"He's got a good home here."

"It's true, but did you expect otherwise?"

"No. Just making an observation." One he had hoped would lead into suggesting another boy would do well here, but her reaction caused him to think now was not the right time.

The kitchen door slapped open.

"Come on, hurry up," Kent said.

Finn turned to see Miss Morton and Kent, hand in hand, headed his way.

Miss Lyster chuckled. "Looks like he's done his chores."

Finn turned the auger as he waited for them to reach him. Was Miss Morton going to forbid him to let Kent hang around? Though he'd done nothing to either encourage or discourage the boy.

She stopped six feet away, still firmly holding Kent's hand. "Mr. Johnson, I would like to thank you for helping Jenny last night. I...we...are most grateful."

"No need for thanks. I just did what needed to be done." He wondered if they could hear the caution in his voice as he waited for what else she had to say.

"Kent is eager to help you, but I am afraid he will be in your way."

"Please, can I help?" Kent leaned forward, held in place only by Miss Morton's firm grip.

The boy was so eager. Seemed a person should take advantage of that. Too often, he saw children sullen and spoiled. More and more he was convinced this was the right place for Eddie.

Planting fence posts was basically a one-man job. However…

"I could use someone like you."

"You're sure?" Miss Morton asked. She looked at the auger, the shovel, the posts, and then Finn. "I truly don't see anything a young boy can do."

"You'd be surprised what a boy can do." He could give her a long list of chores he'd been given. Not that he thought Kent should be made to work so hard. "It would help me a great deal if he held the post for me and helped pack dirt around it."

"See, Auntie. I told you."

Miss Morton released his hand. "Send him in if he gets underfoot."

"I won't. I promise." Kent grabbed the shovel and waited expectantly for working orders.

Finn chuckled. "Nice to see you so eager."

"I'll be watching you." Miss Morton spoke to Kent, but Finn guessed the words were for him.

"Oh, by the way, Hilda asks if you'd like to come in for coffee and cookies." Miss Morton headed for the kitchen.

"Please do," Miss Lyster said, having watched the whole proceedings with a smile. "You didn't come for breakfast, and we expected you."

Kent's shoulders sank. "Aww. I just got here."

Finn pulled out a handful of grass. "Why don't you give this to Bill while I have coffee?" He spoke before he thought through his answer. By rights he should refuse the women, but he hadn't had coffee before he left camp, and longed for a cupful. Before he could say he'd changed his mind Kent took the grass and raced over to where Bill waited, his head up at hearing his name. There was nothing he could do but follow Miss Lyster inside.

As soon as he stepped into the kitchen, Mrs. Meyer grabbed his hand and pumped it.

"Thank you for rescuing our Jenny."

Miss Fisher gave him a shy smile. "Yes, thank you."

Miss Morton held Sally on her hip as she watched the others thank him. He felt her caution.

He was led to the table and coffee and cookies placed before him. He wasn't sure what to make of all the attention and glanced at Miss Lyster. Her green eyes sparkled like sunshine on one of those mineral-rich, green mountain lakes. She was clearly amused.

"We are all most grateful," she said, her tone sincere enough.

He gulped. Lowered his gaze. Sucked back a mouthful of hot coffee that burned his tongue. They all hovered around him, sending his nerves into a frenzied dance. He realized he still wore his hat and snatched it off, suddenly conscious of his need for a haircut. Might not hurt to do something with his beard too.

He lifted a cookie but didn't bite into it, knowing he couldn't swallow past the lump lodged in his throat.

"Girls, we're making him nervous," Miss Lyster said.

The others scurried away to different areas of the

kitchen while Miss Lyster filled a mug and sat across from him.

He returned his cookie to the plate. Having her there did absolutely nothing to relieve his tension. He forced down several mouthfuls of coffee until the cup was drained, then, hoping his movements didn't reveal his hurry, he got to his feet and took two cookies. "Thank you, ladies. Now I best get back to work. Kent will be disappointed if I don't get out there." He managed to keep his stride even all the way back to the hole he'd been digging. Now able to swallow, he ate his two cookies then picked up the auger.

Kent rushed over to ask what he could do.

"Grab me one of those posts."

Kent tried to lift one, staggered under the weight, and settled for dragging it over.

Finn let the boy place the post in the hole. Showed him how to make sure it was straight. "You hold it while I start filling in the hole." He tamped down some dirt then handed Kent the shovel. "I'll hold the post while you shovel in dirt."

Working together, they filled in the hole. Granted, it took twice as long as if he had done it himself, but it was more important to encourage the boy.

"I'll leave you to jump on the dirt and make sure it's good and firm while I start on the next hole."

For the next hour, Kent and Finn worked together before Kent started to lose interest. He sat on the ground while Finn dug another hole and plied Finn with questions about living in the mountains. Was it fun? How did he eat? Who cooked for him? Was he scared of bears?

Finn admitted a touch of relief when Miss Morton called Kent back to the house.

Apart from her earlier visit, Miss Lyster hadn't been out all morning. Finn shifted so he could see the kitchen. Mrs. Meyer was visible at the big worktable. Miss Fisher flitted past the window. He heard the laughter of little Sally and perceived Miss Morton said something. But he neither heard nor saw Miss Lyster. Maybe she was in the dining room. Or she might have gone out the front door. He glanced at what he could see of the dusty street and the town. Two riders trotted by, seemingly headed for Burnsie's store. A solitary man sauntered by as if headed for the wagon train. But no Miss Lyster.

Why was he concerned? Not like it mattered to him one way or the other what she did or where she went. He turned away from the house and bent his back to digging a hole.

The screen door slapped. "I'll be back in time to help with the noon crowd," Miss Lyster called. She crossed to the shed and then emerged with a bucket. She sauntered over to Finn.

"Could you manage without the shovel for a couple of hours? I'm going to dig up some buffalo beans. The last few I got didn't survive, but I'm determined to get a patch going."

"Go ahead. I can dig more holes while you have the shovel." He brought his gaze to her. Her eyes captured the morning sunshine, causing him to think of the green where the meadow touched the trees. For a moment, he couldn't think then remembered she wanted the shovel. "Here you go." He handed it to her.

"Thanks." Singing softly, she left the yard, paused to pat Bill, then proceeded down the street.

Bill trod at her heels.

Finn whistled. "Get back here, long ears."

Bill tipped his ears back and curled his lips, but he stopped and watched Miss Lyster until she turned the corner and was out of sight. Then he moseyed over to the edge of the garden and hung his head like he'd lost his best friend.

The mule was always overly dramatic.

The door opened again, and Kent raced out. "Aunt Delcie says I'm done for the morning." He joined Finn. "Where's the shovel?"

"Miss Lyster is using it."

"Huh." He rocked back and forth a moment then lost interest and went over to Bill. He sat cross-legged in front of the mule and started chattering. Bill listened carefully, nodding from time to time.

Finn smiled. Sometimes a man just had to say his thoughts out loud even if the one listening didn't understand a word. It was enough that Bill remained attentive, almost as if he enjoyed the sound of a human voice.

He looked past Bill and saw the two young men from last night crossing the street and turning down the same path Miss Lyster had taken. Finn watched a moment then made up his mind. The pair might be on innocent business, but he would make sure.

"You stay with Bill," he said to Kent. "I've got something to do." He slipped away, going the same direction the others had gone.

There was no sign of them or of Miss Lyster. He studied the trail and made out the outline of a tiny shoe and went that direction. Near as he could tell, the other two had turned aside, but he intended to make sure she was all right.

He climbed the hill and stopped to study his surroundings. The Porcupine Hills rolled from one into another with copses of trees filling the hollows and crowning the hills. She could be in the trees or have crested one of the hills and gone out of sight. He caught a glimpse of movement and made out her dark green dress, barely visible against the green of the hills. She reached the top of the next hill and was soon out of sight.

He trotted after her. By the time he crested the hill, she had set her pail down and was jabbing the shovel into the ground amidst a patch of bright yellow flowers. He paused to take in the sight. A pretty gal surrounded by flowers, singing as she worked. It was something he knew he would never forget.

Would the memory bless him when he returned to his cabin or would it make him lonely? One thing he was certain of—Eddie would do well with her as his guardian. Somehow he would find a way to bring up the subject.

He started down the hill, then, lest he frighten her, he called, "Thought you could use some help."

She looked up and watched him approach. "This ground is so stubborn. I can't even get near the roots. Here, you try." She practically thrust the shovel at him.

He took it and grinned at her. "You think they'll be less stubborn for me?"

"Maybe you'll have more patience."

He chuckled. "I'll see what I can do." The ground was indeed hard, and it took a lot of effort to cut through the sod. He paused to wipe his brow. Now was the time to mention Eddie. "You must enjoy having Kent and Sally in your home."

"I do. We're all fortunate they can be with us."

Now was the time to point out that Miss Morton wasn't married, and she was guardian to two children. Make Miss Lyster see she could do the same and provide a child with a home even though she wasn't married.

"Is it because of that Mr. Stanley you mentioned that you don't plan to marry?" She was beautiful and hardworking. Any man would be proud to call her his wife.

That wasn't what he'd planned to say. Nor think. But it was more than curiosity that made him ask about the man that made her lips curl. Sort of like how Bill expressed his displeasure.

She looked beyond him, her eyes hard as stone. A shudder crossed her shoulders and she brought her gaze to him. Misery, regret, and anger filled her eyes.

"I suppose you deserve an explanation. Yes, it is because of him and his son. They behaved inappropriately. Abominably."

"I see." Though he did not.

"I doubt you do." Her shoulders rose and fell as she sucked in a deep breath. "What hurts the worst is I didn't see it coming. I had no idea that's what they thought."

Finn nodded. Like Bill, the best he could do was provide a pair of listening ears.

"Isaac Stanley and I were friends. More than friends. We'd spent a great deal of time together, and I assumed he was interested in marriage. But perhaps I was only fooling myself the whole time. Because on this particular day we'd made arrangements to meet friends and go for a walk. I loved spending time with him. It didn't matter who we were with. I knew we would trail behind until we were alone. Isaac would take my hand and tuck it around his arm and pull me close. He'd say sweet things, like he was the luckiest man alive to have me beside him. He'd use any excuse to pull me tighter to his side. Like 'whoops, watch that rock. Wouldn't want you to trip.' We both knew the rock posed no danger."

She gave a little laugh, entirely devoid of amusement. "I was so naïve. Anyway, I was ready early that day, so I decided to go to his house and meet him. I thought we would have that much more time together. Only Isaac wasn't there. His father was. He invited me in. Not realizing he was alone in the house, I went in.

He said Isaac had to run an errand for him and wasn't expected back until after supper. But he—the father— didn't mind entertaining me for a while. He got far too close, and then closer, until his body touched me, pressed against me. I tried to back away, but the table prevented it. I protested. He said, 'Oh, come on. The way you flash those pretty eyes all over the place and sashay around is a clear invitation to every man with eyes. You want a man's attention, and I'm here to give it to you.' He touched me in most inappropriate ways." Her voice caught and she stopped talking.

Finn wasn't sure what to do. Should he offer comfort? Wait for her to go on?

She pressed her fingertips to the corners of her eyes and sniffed.

He couldn't ignore her distress and took her elbow to guide her to a grassy spot. He urged her to sit down. He sat beside her, his elbow pressed to hers. It was the most he could offer in way of comfort and support though he felt an unfamiliar urge to wrap his arms around her and hold her tight. Assure her she was innocent, and the man was a scoundrel.

Air shuddered in and out of her and she began to speak again. "Somehow I managed to push around him and hurry out the door. I ran to the end of the block. I couldn't go home the way I was and alarm my mother. So I went to Delcie's house. She was always glad of my company. She could tell I was upset. I said it was because I'd been expecting to meet Isaac, but his father had sent him on an errand. But she guessed it was more. I don't suppose she could think otherwise when I had to keep fighting back nausea. I felt so dirty. So..." She shuddered, and the way she brought her palm to her mouth, he wondered if she still felt the same sense of nausea.

He pressed his hand to her back. Hoping it wouldn't alarm her. "He was not a nice man."

She nodded. "I couldn't shake off the things Mr. Stanley said to me. Did I flash my eyes and sashay, giving an unintentional message to men? I wouldn't see Isaac after that, and yet I longed for him to tell me everything was all right. He came to the house and asked why I was suddenly so distant. I couldn't tell him. On top of that, every time I turned around, I saw Mr. Stanley watching me. I was afraid of him."

Finn curled his hand into a fist. Why must people do such horrible things to others? Treat fellow human beings in a way he wouldn't treat his mule. Though to be fair, Bill wouldn't stand for it, and he had a killer of a kick. Poor Miss Lyster had no defense.

"Hilda and the others were already making plans to go west. I decided I would go with them. I told Isaac. I thought he might say he'd come too. Instead, he said his pa was right. I was nothing but a tease. Too pretty by far to ever make a good wife. That was the last I saw of him." She faced him, her eyes full of misery.

"You did not deserve to be treated the way they treated you. They are the ones who should feel shame and sorrow. But I don't suppose they do. I'm sorry you went through this. But hear me and hear me good. You are not responsible for their bad behavior."

Her gaze held his unblinkingly. He got the feeling she drank from his words, and he hoped she would let them heal her hurt.

"It's why I've decided I won't marry. Not if someone I think cares about me can treat me like that."

He nodded. "I understand." That's how he felt about how Ethel had treated him. "But don't let them ruin your life."

She shrugged.

He tried to think how to bring the conversation back to children but before he could, she jumped to her feet. "I'm sorry for wasting so much time. I came to dig out buffalo beans not bemoan my past." She grabbed the shovel and jammed it into the place he'd been digging.

He rose more slowly and took the shovel from her, but rather than return to digging he faced her. "You don't need to deprive yourself of all that married life offers."

She blanched, and he knew she thought he was suggesting something other than what he had in mind.

"You can still enjoy having children."

Her color returned. "I am. I enjoy Sally and Kent."

"How would you like a boy of your own?"

Her mouth dropped open. She closed it with an audible click. "Finn, what on earth are you talking about?"

8

*J*enny's mind was in turmoil. She hadn't meant to tell Finn everything about the Stanleys. Just enough to make him see why she'd decided against marriage, though Hilda assured her she'd change her mind when the right man came along. Jenny doubted that.

Finn had listened without judgment. He'd even offered comfort by rubbing her back. Strange that she hadn't felt threatened by that touch.

"What do you mean, I could have a boy of my own?"

"His name is Eddie."

"You have a son?" Why did the idea surprise her? Like he'd said, he was much older than her in more than age. She'd taken it to mean because his childhood had come to an end so early, but perhaps there was more to it.

"Not me. But someone I know is sending her seven-year old son to me to take care of."

She could not find a single coherent thought in her head.

He gave a crooked smile. "I can't take care of a boy. I'm a mountain man."

"It appears she thinks you can." Words suddenly flooded her mind. "Who is this woman, and why is she asking you to take her son?"

He studied the hole he was digging. Ran his hands along the handle of the hoe. Lifted his head and looked past her. His expression revealed nothing beyond a tightening of his mouth.

Assuming he didn't mean to answer her, she bent and examined the plant they were digging out. The roots still clung firmly to the sod.

"She's the Moore's daughter."

Jenny slowly rose at his words and faced him. "The reason you became a mountain man?"

He nodded.

"Care to explain?"

They faced each other across the yellow flowers at their feet.

Something flickered through his eyes. A thousand sorrows and regrets, she decided.

"I guess you need to hear the story. I was taken in by the Moores after my parents died."

She already knew that but if he needed to say it again, she didn't mind.

"Ethel was the same age as me, so we became

friends though she wasn't encouraged to talk with me. Wasting my time, as her father said. Still, she was kind and would, occasionally, bring me little treats. I adored her. I would have given my life for her." He made a derisive sound.

Jenny heard the pain in his tone.

He looked past Jenny as he continued. "At fourteen, I could no longer hide my affection for her. Her parents said it was time for me to be on my own. I told Ethel I would make something of myself and then I'd come back for her. She smiled nicely. I was foolish enough to think she found the idea appealing." He shrugged, though there was more pain than dismissal in the gesture. "I hung around for a bit, working, and tried to see her. Her parents refused to let me, but once I saw her in town and told her how hard I was working. I said I could support her if she married me. She said I didn't have enough money to court a woman let alone marry one. I was shocked. Hurt. But maybe not surprised. All I'd ever heard since the Moores took me in was how little an orphan boy mattered to anyone. So I left to make something of myself. I got on a trail drive. I worked for a rancher. I saved every cent I earned. Two years later I returned and told her how successful I was though I realize now my savings didn't amount to a hill"—he glanced at his feet—"of buffalo beans. She wouldn't even look at me when she said she was engaged to someone. A rich man with a future. She said I didn't have anything to offer her. The money I had saved was a pittance. I had no family. Nothing."

"This Eddie is her son? And she now thinks you have something to offer?" Seemed a little late to come to that conclusion. "Where is her husband?" Was he trying to get the boy away? Did he mean to harm him? A little like Delcie with Sally and Kent? "And why can't she keep the boy?"

"Here. Read her letter." He pulled the envelope from his pocket and handed it to her.

She hesitated to remove the page and look at it. "I'm sure it's private."

"It's about the boy. Read it." His jaw muscles clenched and unclenched. His knuckles were white as he gripped the handle of the shovel. He looked about ready to disintegrate and become part of the soil at their feet, which she didn't care to see happen.

"Very well." She pulled a sheet of fine linen-weave paper from the envelope. Good quality paper. She unfolded it and read aloud.

Dear Finn,

I hope this finds you well. It has taken me some time to track you down. Thanks to Reverend Morgan, I have been able to.

Jenny lifted her gaze to Finn. "Who is Reverend Morgan?"

"He's the preacher back where the Moores live. He was good to me. Taught me that God loved me even if I had no family." A slow, warm smile creased his face.

Goodness, when the man smiled like that it

changed his countenance from that of a mountain man to...to.... She couldn't even think what she meant except it made her mouth go dry.

"He showed me a verse in the Bible that said God was a father to the fatherless. The reverend was good to me. I felt I should let him know I was all right, and so I wrote him."

Jenny sucked moisture into her mouth and bent her head to continue reading.

My husband passed away two years ago. He turned out not to be a good man, given to much drink and growing increasingly belligerent. He died as a result of a fight. But enough about him.

I have a huge favor to ask. Remembering how good and kind you always were and how you always did what was right, I feel certain you will say yes.

I have a son, Eddie. He is seven years old and a dear child. I love him very much. However—and I say this with utmost sorrow—I will be unable to raise him. You see, I am dying.

Jenny gasped. "That's terrible."

Finn's eyes dipped at the corner revealing that he shared her shock. And likely so much more. Sorrow that the woman he had loved and perhaps still did, was dying.

She sniffed at the cruelty of life and continued to read.

I am writing to say I can think of no one I'd sooner have raise my son. You always did your best and were so honorable. You could have stolen from my father, but you didn't.

You could have been bad tempered, but you never were. I know you will give my boy a good home and protect him.

I have made arrangements for him to go to Willow Creek. One thing I ask. Would you please tell him often how much I loved him?

God bless you both.

Sincerely yours,

Ethel

Jenny stared at the words, her throat closed off by her emotions. Then the questions came. "Protect him from what?"

"She doesn't say."

"Where are her parents?"

"I don't know."

"This is all very strange and unusual."

"I can't give him a home."

Jenny shook the piece of paper. "But she says he is on his way." She studied the page before her. There was no date. No return address. She turned back to Finn. Behind the beard and the impassive expression, she saw so much more. Only she couldn't be sure what it was. "Do you regret you didn't stay back to step in when she was widowed?"

It was impossible to misread the shock in his face. "It never crossed my mind. I know she was right. I have nothing to offer a woman. And certainly nothing to offer a child."

"It would appear she doesn't agree. Why can't you give him a home?"

"I'm a mountain man. I live in a cabin by myself.

It's no place for a child." He jabbed the shovel into the ground with enough force to send a shudder through his body. As if the conversation was over. Then he paused and looked at her. "Would you give him a home?"

Their gazes held, his pleading, hers likely confused and uncertain, as that was how she felt. It wasn't that the idea of having the child didn't appeal, but to think of him being rejected by the only person who had any connection to his family felt wrong.

"Finn, how can you say no to the child? You know what it's like to be orphaned. To not be important to anyone. You could take him with you. Or choose to live somewhere else."

"I have nothing to offer him." The words, rather than sounding like a reasonable defense, sounded like defeat.

"You keep saying that. Why are you letting something someone said to you years ago still bother you, especially when you know it isn't true?"

His eyes widened and then narrowed. "I might ask you the same thing. Why are you letting what Mr. Stanley said affect you so strongly when you know it isn't true?"

She backed away, stung by how he'd turned the conversation into an attack. Realizing she still held the letter, she thrust it at him. "Take it."

Without breaking away from her gaze, he reached for it. His hand encircled hers. Warm. Strong. Protective. So many things that ached at the depths of her heart.

Her breath caught in her throat. Her pulse beat hard against her ribs. Neither of them jerked away.

"I did not mean to offend you." His voice echoed in her hollow head. Why couldn't she regain her senses?

She scrubbed her lips together and sought in vain for a reply.

He opened his hand, plucked the letter from her fingers, folded the page, slipped it into the envelope, and returned it to his pocket.

She watched each movement, her thoughts and limbs frozen in place.

He grabbed the shovel and attacked the flowers at their feet.

Jenny backed away, unable to tear her gaze from him. What had happened? Why was she so affected by an accidental touch?

She rubbed her hands together but could not shed herself of the feeling that something significant had just occurred.

He squatted down and eased loose a clump of roots and flowers.

She shook off the confusion that claimed her brain, grabbed the bucket, and took it over to where he worked. Together they put the bundle of roots and dirt into it. Together they straightened and faced each other. She pulled her gaze away but just as quickly returned it. Heat mounted in her cheeks. What was wrong with her? One would think she'd never met a man's eyes before the way looking at Finn had her all confused.

She grabbed the handle of the pail. "I need to get these home and planted." The pail was surprisingly heavy, and she grunted.

"I'll take it. You carry the shovel."

She nodded and stepped away before he took the handle of the pail then realized how jittery she was and forced herself to slow down.

Not until they had begun the trek back to town did she realize she hadn't given him an answer to his request. And he hadn't asked again. Maybe she had offended him, and he had changed his mind. Or he might be reconsidering his request. Perhaps her words would force him to stop believing what this Ethel had said to him.

Would they affect him enough he would choose to give the boy a home?

FINN WAS silent as they headed back to town, but his mind had more words bursting at the seams than he'd had in the previous two years combined. He'd asked her to take Eddie and she hadn't agreed. Not that she'd refused. Just said he should keep the boy. Did she really think he could provide a home for him? That it was only Ethel's saying he had nothing to offer that made him think he couldn't? But it was so much more than the hurt lingering from those words. It was more than the distance he'd put between himself and others. The fact was he lived in a cabin away from civilization. Away from people. A child did not fit into that life, and he didn't know that he could live somewhere else. What would he do? "How can I live somewhere else?"

"Didn't you say you worked on a ranch? You could do that again. Maybe buy your own ranch? Of course, I don't know if that's possible, but I'm certain you can work something out if you so desire. Do you?"

Did he? "It's not that simple. I don't know anything about families. Or being a father. All I know is work, and that's not all a boy should know."

"I'd say that's a step in the right direction. Knowing what changes you need to make is sometimes all it takes to start making them."

He shook his head. How could she begin to understand? "An orphan boy doesn't eat at the table with the family. He does his chores quickly and without complaining even if he's sick. And if he complains the man can whip it out of him or send him away."

Miss Lyster had stopped walking to stare at him. "Is that how things were? You poor child."

"I had another choice. I could change my attitude. By the time he got done laying out the options and the consequences, I figured any kid with half a brain in his head would choose to get along. Besides, Ethel pointed out that my parents would be disappointed to learn I was being stupid and bullheaded. That helped me as much as anything."

Miss Lyster rested the shovel on the ground and

placed a warm and tender hand on his arm. Was she not aware of how her touch affected him? When his hand had accidently cupped hers as he reached for the letter, his heart had stalled. Every nerve in his body had snapped like static electricity. And now her hand on his arm had his insides quivering. Had she any idea how long he'd gone without a gentle, loving touch? Since his mother had died, surely. And he barely remembered her, though he thought she had hugged him and kissed him. Or it could be he simply kept that dream alive to sustain himself during the lonely, fearful nights of being an orphan boy.

A lump the size of a full-grown cat filled his lungs until he couldn't breathe. Couldn't think. Couldn't remember who he was, where he was. All that existed, at this point in time, was the warmth of her hand and the welcome in her eyes.

There was something wrong with that idea, but he couldn't think what. Couldn't think anything at the moment.

"Your parents loved you, didn't they?"

Her question jerked him back to reality and he nodded. "Far as I know. I can't rightly remember much about them."

"I think Ethel gave you good advice when she said you should do what your parents would want. Finn, what would they want you to do?"

Her soft words slipped into his heart. "I don't know. All I hear is Mr. Moore's voice telling me to work hard and keep my thoughts to myself."

"What do you think Reverend Morgan would say?"

Reverend Morgan? The one man who had treated him like a real person. "He always had lots to say, but I don't recall much." That wasn't entirely the truth. The man's encouragement and admonition had often helped Finn. But how did that change what was now?

"Finn, maybe it's time to stop thinking like an orphan boy."

Her words hammered against the rock-solid encasement of his heart. That shell was all that held him together. If it shattered, he would shatter too, so he dismissed her words and resumed walking toward town.

Miss Lyster fell into step beside him, swinging the shovel in time to their steps. "Thanks for helping dig out the flowers."

"You're welcome." If she was ready to leave off their discussion, he was too. He would find another time and manner of asking her to give Eddie a home. Because he knew he couldn't do it. It wouldn't be fair to the boy.

They reached town, crossed the street to her garden.

Both children sat in front of Bill, playing some sort of game in which Bill was a part.

Finn laughed though he wondered if a thread of tension could be heard. It wasn't easy to push aside the confusion of the last hour. "Is he keeping them amused, or are they entertaining him?"

She chuckled. "I'd say it was both." She tipped her

head sideways to study Finn. "Seems your mule likes children."

He knew what she was doing. Hoping that comparing him to his mule would make him feel guilty, but it didn't. "Bill likes the company of anyone."

Her eyebrows rose. "No doubt he would enjoy getting to know Eddie."

Finn wouldn't look at her. Instead, he lifted the bucket of flowers. "Where do you want these?"

She indicated a spot near the chicken yard, and he carried the bucket there.She followed.

"I'll dig a hole." He reached for the shovel.

She pulled it closer to her body and lifted her eyes to his. Green as winter-clad pine, bright as sunshine on a lake, challenging as a strong wind. "Are you offering help because you think you need to work?"

He withdrew his hand. Her question startled him. Unsettled him. He didn't often analyze his choices. In fact, never. "Do I need an explanation for helping?"

She waited.

"Isn't it enough that you need a hole dug and I can do it?"

She shook her head. "I am capable of digging a hole." She indicated the garden and swept her hand from one side to the other. "I planted all this myself."

He knew what she'd done and how much work it entailed. He'd taken it all in the first time he was in the garden. Wild rosebushes along one side next to where he would build the fence. Some kind of plant with round, wavy leaves along the pathway. Other plants he didn't recognize in rows along the house and in bunches in the corner. "Some of the plants look eager to grow, others hang their leaves like unhappy children."

Their gazes collided at his words.

Acknowledgement of his meaning flickered through her eyes. "With water, protection, and proper care, they will all soon look healthy."

"I hope you're right. But in the end, they are plants and can be replaced." He took the shovel from her. She gave no resistance. Perhaps distracted by his words. He dug a hole larger than the clump of dirt then stepped back to let her place the plant.

He returned to digging holes for the fence posts but his attention was on Miss Lyster as she patted dirt around the plant, carried water to it, then took her shears to it and pruned off the flowers and a good deal of the leaves. Guess she thought that would improve the plant's chances of surviving.

He had roots too. His little cabin up on the mountain nestled near a lake, almost hidden by the surrounding spruce trees. The thought of uprooting his life, transplanting it somewhere else, enduring the pruning and adjusting, did not appeal.

Nor did the idea of planting someone else in his life.

He considered each of the ladies who ran the diner and bakery. They had been kind with their thanks for rescuing Jenny but Mrs. Meyer, with her brisk manner, made him nervous. Miss Fisher could hardly meet his eyes, as if she either feared him or disliked him for no reason. He'd never be able to talk to her. And Miss Morton made no secret of the fact she didn't care for him. That left him with one option. Persuade Miss Lyster to take Eddie.

9

———

*J*enny sat back on her heels and looked at the plant now in her garden. But her thoughts were far from the buffalo bean and her hopes for it. They were scattered like leaves in the fall, blowing from one thing to another.

Finn. Eddie. Ethel. Finn's reluctance to take the son of his lost love.

Jenny jolted at the last thought. Was it because the boy would remind him of Ethel that he didn't want to give him a home? That made sense in a sad sort of way.

Sad for Finn. Sad for Eddie if Finn couldn't look at him without regret.

It bothered her to think of a seven-year old child wanted by no one. Except he would be welcome here. It would be nice for Kent to have another boy around. They could be like brothers. Jenny thought of mothering the boy and smiled as she thought of reading him bedtime stories and tucking him in at night, taking him on picnics, making him special treats.

Yes, she'd like to have a little boy to love.

Finn should not deny himself the same pleasure.

She went over the things he'd said. Losing his parents at a young age, barely able to remember them, being told he was an orphan boy, to work hard and keep his feelings and thoughts to himself, and then having the woman he loved tell him he had nothing to offer. No wonder he'd retreated to the mountains.

He needed to leave that hurtful past behind and rejoin the world.

A Bible verse sprang to mind. *This one thing I do, forgetting those things which are behind, and reaching forth unto those things which are before, I press toward the mark for the prize of the high calling of God in Christ Jesus.*

Was that what God wanted for Finn? What if God had directed Ethel to send Eddie to Finn as part of getting him to leave the past and reach for the future? She made up her mind right there on her knees before an uprooted plant. She would not interfere in God's plans by agreeing to take the boy. Instead, she would find ways to encourage Finn to see this as an opportunity for himself.

She'd already tried and failed and had no idea what else she could do. Other than pray for God's guidance. Another Bible verse sprang to her mind. *I will instruct thee and teach thee in the way which thou shalt go: I will guide thee with mine eye.*

Lord, I don't know what to say or do to help Finn. Please instruct me and guide me.

She remained with her head bowed for a few seconds than straightened with a sigh. Of course she hadn't expected to hear God whisper instructions in her ears or give her an idea so grand and glorious she knew it must be from Him. Except maybe she had.

She looked around. Nothing had changed. Finn continued to dig holes and put in posts, keeping his back to her. The children still played with Bill. Maybe God didn't need her help. Maybe He wanted her to leave Finn alone to sort things out on his own.

She put away the bucket and went inside to wash her hands and help with meal preparations. Delcie called the children in and fed them before customers arrived.

Jenny stuffed back the ache she felt for a little boy who would soon be an orphan. Perhaps already was and needed someone to love and care for him. She would gladly be the one to give him that but not when she had this feeling that Finn should be the one to do it. God's way, not hers. She must remember that.

The wagon train still camped down by the creek, and a dozen or so of the people came for dinner. Some purchased bread before they left. A few regular customers came in for bread.

The dining room emptied. The children did their chores then ran outside to talk to Bill.

Hilda handed plates to each of the women. "Ve can eat now."

Jenny took her plate and looked out the window. "Shall I invite him in to eat with us?"

Both Laura and Delcie looked unhappy about the possibility.

"He should have come in when the others were here," Laura said.

"Ve vill be hospitable," Hilda said. "Yes, tell him to come in."

Jenny did not wait to hear what the others would say but went to the door and called to Finn. "Come and eat."

He hesitated. Then slowly put down the shovel and made his way to the house. He paused inside the door and took off his hat.

She pointed him toward the basin of warm water she had poured for him.

Looking as comfortable as a bird amidst half a dozen hungry cats, he washed, smoothed his hair, then took the plate she handed him. He stood back, waiting until everyone else had filled their plates from the pots on the stove before he helped himself then stepped toward the dining room.

Sitting at the table with the others, Jenny saw his intention. "Join us." She indicated the chair across the corner to her right.

He stared at her and then the empty chair. "I won't intrude." And took another step toward the door.

"Nonsense."

"You are most velcome to sit with us."

Neither Laura nor Delcie looked welcoming but

they were polite enough to keep their feelings to themselves.

Finn perched on the chair as Hilda asked the blessing then kept his head down as he ate.

Jenny wanted to tell the other ladies that Finn wasn't so shy and awkward when he was with her. When it was just the two of them, he met her eyes and answered her questions. She had a burning urge to shake him. Tell him not to be so guarded around people. No one was going to scold him or rebuke him.

He finished before the others and got to his feet. "Thank you for the meal and please excuse me." He was out the door before any of them could respond.

"Well, he certainly is a strange one," Delcie said.

Jenny rushed after him, catching him as he began to dig another hole. She grabbed his elbow. "Why did you act like that?"

He met her eyes then jerked away. "I don't know what you're talking about." He twisted on the auger. It skipped and bounced. He started again.

"I think you do. My friends have welcomed you and treated you kindly and yet you act like they are the same as Mr. Moore. They aren't going to scold you or send you to bed without your supper."

She knew from the way he flinched that Mr. Moore had done that enough times to make a lasting impression on Finn.

"Finn, how long will you continue to act like an orphan boy? You are a man. Free to do as you please."

"Yes, I am."

"You don't sound convinced."

He paused and leaned on the auger. "I don't feel the need to convince anyone."

"Except yourself." The words were angry, frustrated, ineffective weapons from her mouth.

He turned the auger. "I am a mountain man. I live alone."

He couldn't have been any more dismissive. Couldn't have made it any plainer that he didn't intend to change his mind. Homeless little boy or not.

She tossed her hands upward at the futility of trying to make him see things differently. Why did she even care? She went back to the house and stormed out the front door before her friends could ask her what was wrong. In the street, she stopped. If she went to the right, she'd reach the creek where the wagon train still camped. With no desire to encounter the young men who had bothered her the night before, she went to the left and walked until the town fell behind her.

After a bit, calmness returned. Nothing she said or did dented the armor Finn wore around his heart. If he was to change, see his potential, see that a little boy needed him, it would have to be God's work not hers.

She walked for an hour and reached some trees where she sat down to think. She wished she'd brought her Bible so she could search for guidance and encouragement. She prayed for strength and wisdom for herself, for God to work in Finn's life and for Eddie to be given a loving home.

Then, realizing how long she'd been gone, she hurried back to the diner to help.

As she prepared vegetables, she could see Finn through the kitchen window. Still at work, but she did not go out to speak to him. Not that she thought he would notice or care.

* * *

FINN WORKED ON THE FENCE. The children did not come out and talk to him. Miss Lyster didn't even go to her garden. He was aware she was angry at him though he couldn't understand why. Even Bill crossed the street and munched on grass a distance away as if to say he didn't care for Finn's company either.

I don't care, Finn told himself. He'd said he'd build a fence and he would do it. While he waited for Eddie.

What was he going to do about the boy? Why had Ethel asked him to take her son? The request had disrupted his peaceful life.

So had Miss Lyster with all her fine talk of forgetting the things he'd been told as a boy. She had no idea of how words repeated often enough became a voice he heard inside his head.

Still, he had no wish to make her angry and even less to have her not speak to him again.

But what was done was done and he couldn't see any way of undoing it.

He could apologize but he couldn't change his

mind. He had nothing to offer a child except a lonely, isolated cabin.

His arms ached. His shirt was soaked with sweat as the afternoon wore on.

Bill made a funny little sound and trotted down the street and out of sight.

What was the silly critter up to this time? He better make sure it wasn't mischief. Finn left his work and slipped out to the sidewalk to watch his mule.

Miss Lyster came down the street. Where had she been? Did she know it wasn't safe with the wagon train still camped by the creek?

Bill trotted up to her and she laughed and scratched behind his ear.

Finn hurried back to the fence before either of them noticed him. Everyone liked Bill. Bill liked everyone. Not that Finn wanted to be scratched behind his ears.

Trouble was, he didn't know what he wanted.

Except some peace and quiet. And the lumber to finish this fence.

He worked until he saw people from the wagon train coming for supper then put away his tools and hurried over to the store.

"How do," Burnsie called.

"You get that lumber yet?" Finn was sure he knew the answer, as he hadn't seen any freight wagons arrive in town.

"Nope. Have to wait for someone to bring it."

"You got a wagon?" He knew the answer to that as well.

"Yup." Burnsie studied him like he'd suddenly grown three heads. "Why you asking questions you knows the answer to?"

"Just been thinking. How about if I take the wagon and go to the fort and get the supplies?"

Burnsie nodded. "You could do that, I suppose."

"Good. I'll leave in the morning."

"Suit yerself, though why youse in such a hurry to get thet fence built when you could be enjoyin' good company and good food, beats me. But like I say, suit yerself."

Satisfied that the trip would provide him with an escape, Finn returned to setting in posts.

Escape? His suddenly active mind demanded, what did he need escape from?

Everything. Everyone.

The answer left him empty and ...

Sad? How could he be sad? He had exactly what he wanted in his life. His cabin up the mountain. Bill for company should he get lonesome.

A picture came to mind—Bill trotting to meet Miss Lyster. Something about that scene filled Finn with an unfamiliar feeling. Not one he was going to probe at.

Kent was sent out to call him in for supper. It was Mrs. Meyer who handed him his plate and pointed him toward the table. Miss Lyster sat kitty-corner to him, exactly where she'd been at dinnertime, but she didn't look his way. Not even once. Not that he noticed or cared.

The children ate with them, and they chattered enough to fill in the silences. Mrs. Meyer asked him a few questions and tried, without success, to get the others to contribute to a conversation.

"I won't be here tomorrow," Finn said as Mrs. Meyer served him a generous slice of apple pie.

That brought all eyes to him.

"I'm going to Fort Macleod to pick up the lumber for the fence."

Kent bounced forward. "How long you gonna be? Can I go with you?"

"No, you can't," Miss Morton said.

"Aww. I never get to do anything fun." He slumped in his chair, his chin almost resting on his chest.

It would have been pleasant to have the boy's company on the trip, and Finn would have enjoyed showing him around the fort. When no one repeated Kent's other question, Finn said, "I'll be gone two days." He ate his pie and excused himself from the table to return to his work. Three more posts to set and he'd be ready to put on the cross pieces and then the uprights.

It was dusk before he finished and put away the tools. He lingered near the toolshed, but no one came out to bid him good-bye. Not that he expected anyone would. Nor was he disappointed no one had.

He crossed the yard toward the street, pausing in front of the window. Mrs. Meyer was busy in the kitchen and waved to him. None of the others were visible. He reached the street and called Bill.

The mule came to him but pressed against his chest, making it impossible to move forward.

"What do you want, old friend?"

Bill lifted his head to look toward the window.

"You like them, don't you?"

Bill continued his study.

"Well, don't get too fond of them. We'll be going back to the cabin. Alone."

Bill blew steam out his nostrils.

"You'll get used to it again."

They made their way to the campsite and hunkered down over a campfire. It had been a strange day. At least up on the mountain, he more or less knew what to expect. The weather and the animals were far more predictable than people.

He'd thought of things and people and events today that he'd pushed from his mind for so long he was surprised their memory still existed.

Except Reverend Morgan. He'd often recalled his words in his lonely years on the mountain. The man had always been kind and encouraging, as good a friend as Finn ever had.

A father to the fatherless.

Don't let anyone tell you who you are or what you can be. You choose that.

People don't realize how hurtful carelessly spoken words can be. Don't let yourself be a victim of them. He jolted to attention. He'd never understood what that meant until now. Perhaps it was as Miss Lyster said. He was letting unkind words control him. Huh. He'd never thought of that.

He sank back over his knees. Miss Lyster's words weren't unkind, but they were certainly unsettling, and he didn't much care for being unsettled.

More of Reverend Morton's word filled his thoughts.

Change is hard but sometimes necessary. Like squeezing infection from a wound so it will heal.

But Finn had no wounds. Only an encased heart, and it didn't hurt. No need to consider change.

Don't be afraid to trust people. Just be sure they are trustworthy. But remember, sometimes you need to take a chance if you want to have friends.

Finn shook his head. Friends could be fickle. Hurtful. Growing up, he'd tried to make friends with other children, but they didn't see him as equal. Working as a cowboy, he'd learned that most of the others preferred their lonely lives. Blaze Hooper and his brothers were the closest he could call friends.

This one thing I do, forgetting those things which are behind, and reaching forth unto those things which are before.

Finn was back on the Moore farm, Reverend Morgan sitting beside him on a chunk of log, a Bible open between them as he read the verse aloud.

"Finn, never let the past decide your future. God has great things in store for you."

Finn stared into the flames. Up on the mountain,

he had many times thanked God for providing him with the means and strength to build a solid cabin and for the peace of the woods and water. It was all he expected to have in life. All he deserved. Why, then, didn't he feel satisfied?

He pulled his Bible from his saddlebag and opened it. Blaze had told him how God used His written word to direct a man. Finn smiled as he recalled how Blaze had flipped the Bible open to Proverbs chapter three and pointed out the scripture. *In all thy ways acknowledge him, and he shall direct thy paths.* He opened the Bible to the same place and read the verse. His eyes naturally followed to the next line. *Be not wise in thine own eyes.* The words coiled inside his head, but he couldn't think what they meant. Shouldn't a man be wise in the way he lived? Shouldn't he learn from the past and not repeat its mistakes?

The reverend's words echoed. *Never let the past decide your future.*

It was all far too confusing. He couldn't wait to finish the fence and get back to his peaceful life.

The fire had died down. Finn spread his bedroll and lay on it.

His view of the future was limited to going to the fort. Getting Miss Lyster to give Eddie a home and then making his way back to his cabin.

Back. Did he want to go backward or forward?

Did it matter what he decided? Would anyone care?

10

As Jenny washed the dishes the next morning, her attention went often to the window and the scene beyond. The stark fence posts were a constant reminder of the man who had placed them there. She'd been serving breakfast in the dining room when she'd seen him depart on a wagon, Bill trotting along behind. Of course he hadn't come to say goodbye. She hadn't expected it. Not after how studiously she'd avoided looking at him or talking to him last night. It was only because she had decided not to offer help or advice. God would have to convince him he had no choice but to give Eddie a home. She thought she might be able to aid the process by being so distant he wouldn't feel free to ask her again to become Eddie's guardian.

He'd be gone two days. That would give God plenty of time to work in his heart.

She smiled at the hope of seeing the change. In the meantime, she meant to keep busy. She removed all the tablecloths in the dining room and washed them, hanging them in the sunshine to dry. She swept every corner and crevice in the room then got down on her hands and knees with a bucket of hot, soapy water and scrubbed the boards until not a speck of dirt remained.

She barely finished, the floor still damp, new tablecloths on the tables just in time for the noon meal. For the next hour she kept busy serving meals, stirring gravy, bringing dirty dishes back to the kitchen.

The women finally sat down for their own meal.

"You've been going like a whirlwind," Laura observed, with nothing but kindness in her voice.

"I feel like I've been slacking the last few days."

"Of course you haven't," Hilda assured her. "Ve all do our share."

Delcie added her agreement. "The garden is important for both our business and our survival."

"Which reminds me, I should check on it this afternoon." There was always weeding, watering, and tending to do.

She helped clean the kitchen then went out to the garden. Her glance went to the clump of buffalo beans Finn had helped her dig out. She stared at where they had been. They were gone. "Oh no." She hurried over. Hoofprints informed her what had happened. Someone's horse had gotten in and eaten her plant. A noise came from behind the chicken house, and she rushed around, hoping to find the animal responsible.

She skidded to a halt, and her fists uncurled. "Bill! What are you doing here?" She looked around for Finn. No sign of him. She crossed her arms and studied the mule. A leaf hung from his lip. "You ate my plant."

He nodded his head.

"You needn't be so pleased with yourself. Where's Finn?" As if the mule could tell her! Had Bill returned of his own accord? Had Finn encountered trouble? How was she to know? "You stay here and stay out of my garden." She dashed across the street to the store.

"Howdy, miss," Burnsie greeted. "Mail just came." He held a handful of letters and newspapers. "What can I do for ya?"

"Finn's mule is in my yard. Has something happened to Finn?"

"Don't think so. Rider with mail spoke to him not long ago. That old mule probably decided he didn't want to go with Finn and came back on his own. He's kinda independent minded, ya know."

"I guess." It wasn't exactly reassuring, but there was little more she could do. "Thanks. Sorry for bothering you."

"No bother." He returned to sorting through the mail. "Hang on. There's something here for you." He held out a white envelope.

She took it. The return address informed her it was from her parents. She thanked Burnsie, tucked it in her pocket, and hurried back to the garden hoping to get there before Bill did any more damage.

The mule waited where she'd left him. They stared at each other. "What am I supposed to do with you?"

Bill wagged his head back and forth and made a strange sound that almost resembled laughter.

"Well, you can't wander free and snack on my garden." She had no place to pen him. Could she tie him?

Kent joined her. "I could watch him for you."

"Perfect. Can you make sure he stays out of the garden?"

"Yup. Come on, Bill." He waved for Bill to follow him and they went past the garden area, past where the fence would be, and several yards beyond to a grassy area.

Delcie joined Jenny. "Why is that animal here?"

"I don't know. Burnsie said he's independent. I take that to mean he does what he wants."

"Great."

"Do you mind if Kent watches him, keeps him out of the garden?"

Delcie laughed. "You think Kent can stop him from doing exactly what he wants?"

"Probably not, but he seems content to stay with him. Maybe he wants Kent's company."

"Maybe. But what are you going to do with him tonight?"

"Good question. Burnsie has a pen behind the store. I'll ask if he can stay there."

"Why not leave him there now?"

Jenny watched Bill and Kent interacting. "He'd be lonely and discontent. Might lead to trouble."

"Very well. Kent seems to like his company. So long as they don't get into mischief…"

"I'll keep an eye on them while I work in the garden."

Both women went back to their work. The sun was warm, the birds sang from the nearby trees, and Kent's voice carried like a distant whisper as Jenny bent to weeding. And tried not to worry about Finn's safety. Burnsie wasn't concerned and he knew the situation better than she did. Yet that did not give her complete relief. *God, keep him safe. Work in his heart so he will willingly, eagerly become a father to Eddie.*

Noon approached, and Jenny left the garden to help in the kitchen. She served meals to the travelers and learned the wagon train would leave in the morning. It would cut down on their customers, but she wouldn't be sorry to see that pair of young men gone. They came for every meal and eyed her hungrily. She figured only Finn's presence made them behave and with him gone…

Kent said Bill was content to stay in the grassy spot. "He can see us, so he knows it's all right."

Jenny and the others exchanged amused glances, but no one asked Kent how he knew what the mule thought. Let the boy enjoy his imagination.

She helped clean the kitchen then headed for the

garden. That's when she remembered her letter and sat on the chair beside the house to open it and read it.

Her parents were well and missed her. They hoped everything was good with Jenny. Moving west was a big step. There was news of the neighbors and community. The next words caught in her craw.

Your father overhead Isaac say a derogatory thing about you. We were both much surprised at the vindictiveness of his words. Your father confronted Isaac and told him to keep his mouth shut in the future. Is this why you decided to leave so suddenly? Your father believes it is and is set on righting the wrong. I fear if he does anything, it might lead to a feud.

Jenny slapped the page to her knee. That was the very reason she hadn't told her parents what happened. She did not want her parents involved in a fight with the Stanleys. She'd convinced them she was in need of some adventure in her life.

If only her brother was home. But Ralph had gone south and gotten a job on a cattle ranch. She had half a mind to write him and tell him the facts. She sighed. She didn't want him to get involved in her troubles either, but how she longed to see him. He'd been her friend and protector when she was growing up, and she missed him so much.

She sprang to her feet and stuffed the letter back in her pocket. She would write a response immediately and tell her parents not to be bothered with the Stanleys.

"I have to write back home," she said by way of

explanation to the others as she hurried into the kitchen and right to the desk in the corner where they had a little sitting area. She got out pen, ink, and paper and carefully wrote a letter, filling it with news about the business, the mountain man and his mule, and the wagon train passing through. She ended with the words she had prepared about Isaac.

He is a troubled young man. But pay him no attention. Nothing bad he says about me is true, and so no need to spring to my defense. I am happy here and find myself leading a useful and satisfying life.

She ended the letter then pulled out a second sheet of paper and wrote to Ralph also, telling him about the business she was now part of, the countryside and the mountain man. She closed with words of affection and a wish she might see him soon. *If you can tear yourself away from those cows, I'd love to see you. Your devoted sister, Jen-jen.*

Sealing the envelopes, she went across the store and affixed postage.

"They'll go out today or tomorrow," Burnsie assured her.

She asked if she could pen Bill in his corral for the night, and Burnsie agreed.

Content with having dealt with two matters, she returned to the garden and spent the rest of the day weeding and watering.

At evening, she took the mule across to the pen behind the store and shut him in. "You stay there, and I'll get you in the morning." She glanced back just before she turned out of sight of the animal. He stared after her, looking sad. No doubt missing his owner.

She shook her head. Bill didn't miss Finn any more than she did. Her steps brisk, she returned home.

THE NEXT MORNING, she did all her usual activities, but the morning had more hours than work. Hilda had mixed up another batch of bread and turned it out onto the table to knead it.

"Let me," Jenny said. She scrubbed her hands and tackled the massive pile of dough, lifting it, turning it, slapping it against the table, and driving her knuckles deep into the sticky mass. She grunted as she repeated the steps, over and over.

Hilda chuckled. "My mother vould call that angry kneading."

Jenny paused, glanced up, and saw all three of her friends watching her with varying degrees of amusement on their faces.

Delcie's eyebrows rose. "Or is she missing someone?"

"Me? Of course not. It's just…just. Well, if you must know, I've had a troubling letter from my parents." She dove her fists into the dough.

Laura rubbed her gentle hand along Jenny's arm. "I hope there's nothing wrong."

Jenny swallowed hard as tears rushed to her eyes. She wouldn't say it, but it wasn't just Isaac. It was so many things. Bill out there without his owner. Eddie needing a father. Finn perhaps in trouble. And so stubborn. What would it take for him to accept that he could and should take Eddie? The poor little boy. She sniffed. "It's just Isaac acting like a spoiled child and upsetting my father."

"How selfish and unkind." Delcie had no patience with men doing cruel things.

Laura rubbed Jenny's arm again. "You are well rid of that man. He has shown his true colors."

Hilda clapped her hands. "Some men are good. Some are bad. Ve need to ask God to show us vhat each is, but, girls, please remember, not all are bad. My Gerhard vas a good man, God rest his soul."

Jenny's own troubles were instantly forgotten in light of Hilda's pain. She'd lost her husband and her parents on the trip across the ocean. She was expecting a baby at the time and later lost the child. Isaac was but an annoyance in comparison.

"You are right, and we need to keep that in mind. My brother is also a good man, as is my father," Jenny said. What category did Finn fit into? It didn't matter for her sake, but it did for Eddie's. She didn't know the man well, but in her heart, felt him to be honorable. Wasn't that what Ethel had said in her letter, and she had known him for years?

They all returned to their work. Soon enough it was time for the noon meal, though they had fewer today as the wagon train had left, taking all the baked bread with them.

The afternoon stretched out like a long winter

night. She'd brought Bill back first thing in the morning, and he remained in the grassy area even without Kent watching him. Her gaze went to the empty spot where the buffalo beans had been ripped out.

"I'm going to find a plant to replace the one Bill ate."

No one objected. They would each enjoy the quiet afternoon in their own way.

She went to her corner of the bedroom, got a bag to hang over her shoulder, and put her Bible in it. She'd been longing to sit outside and enjoy some time alone. At the shed, she got a bucket and shovel then headed up the hill. The sunshine felt good. The blue sky filled her with joy. Trees, flowers, and birds everywhere. What a beautiful country.

She climbed one hill after another, finding something over each to rejoice in. A movement to her right stopped her in her tracks. She held her breath as a deer and twin fawns tiptoed out and crossed the meadow.

Something moved at her feet and she screamed and jumped back. Seeing it was only a rabbit, she laughed. It had been hiding from her.

She continued on to the next hill, driven by a curiosity to see what was over it. At the top, she put down the shovel and pail and lifted her arms in the air. Never had she felt so free. To her right, down the slope a bit, a patch of flowers beckoned. More yellow buffalo beans, dainty bluebells, glorious red brush-looking flowers she didn't recognize.

She carried her belongings that direction and settled down in the warm grass, surrounded by the beauty of God's creation. She pulled out her Bible, turned to the Psalms, and began to read. Verse after verse, chapter after chapter, her soul was refreshed, her inner resolve strengthened. Why did she let things bother her so much when she had a God of might and majesty who loved her and had promised to be with her always?

She shivered and glanced up. Black clouds scuttled across the sky. She leapt to her feet, grabbed her shovel, and tackled digging out the buffalo bean plant. Without Finn to help, the digging was hard and time consuming. The clouds gathered. The wind increased. But she would not go without the plant she had come for.

Finally, she could lift the clump of dirt and roots from the ground and shove it into the pail. Struggling under the weight of the bucket and the awkwardness of trying to carry the shovel too, she climbed the hill and headed for home.

She stopped at the top of the rise and looked around. Green hill after green hill. They all looked the same. Nothing looked familiar. What direction had she come? What direction to take back to town?

Forcing herself to be calm she looked at the ground, hoping to see her tracks, but the wind blew the blades of grass into a wild dance and she could make out nothing. *Think. Think. You climbed this hill. Where did you come from?*

Down the hill. She ran, afraid and anxious. Her feet caught on the tangled grass. Her shovel went one direction, the bucket another, and she sailed forward, landing hard.

Everything went black.

* * *

FINN STOPPED at the store to inform Burnsie he was back and to unload the supplies he'd picked up for the storekeeper.

"Yer mule's been here," Burnsie said.

"Crazy old critter wouldn't be persuaded to stay with me."

"He's been hanging about over there." Burnsie jabbed his finger in the general direction of the diner.

Finn guessed that's where Bill would go. "He been behavin'?"

"Like an angel."

Finn chuckled to think of Bill described in those terms.

They carried in Burnsie's things then Finn drove the wagon across the street to unload the lumber close to where he would build the fence.

Kent trotted out to talk to him. "Bill's been here, in case you was worried about him."

"I see him." The mule gave Finn a quick glance then returned to munching grass. "You been taking care of him?"

"Yup. Me and him is friends." Kent hooked his thumbs in his waistband and leaned back.

Finn kept back a grin. "Thanks for doing that."

Kent eyed him. "You got a haircut."

"Thought it was time." He'd had his beard trimmed to a neat one inch as well. It felt kind of good. He glanced toward the kitchen window. Saw one of the women pass by. Looked to be Hilda. But no one came to greet him. By no one, he meant Jenny. He'd spent a lot of time on his trip thinking of Jenny and what she'd said. Not that he expected she would be anxious to ask him about his trip and certainly not about his thoughts.

He returned to stacking the lumber from the wagon on the ground.

All afternoon, he'd watched the clouds gathering in the west. And now they began to scuttle across the sky. "Gonna rain," he observed.

Kent looked at the sky. "Yup."

The wind increased and turned cold. The clouds hung heavy and dark. He shivered. "You best get inside before you get wet."

Kent sauntered away. A drop of cold rain hit him, and he ran for the house.

Finn chuckled. It was fine for Kent to pretend he was too grown-up to care about a little thing like the weather, until it turned nasty.

Finn's belongings were in the wagon, and he pulled out his slicker and put it on then returned to unloading the lumber.

The door of the kitchen opened. He grinned. He'd wondered how long it would be before Miss Lyster confronted him. He kind of looked forward to hearing what she'd have to say. No doubt something about how he should give Eddie a home. Or tell him he needed to forget the lessons he'd learned at the Moore farm. Easy for her to say. Harder to do. He'd rehearsed how he would explain that.

He turned slowly. It wasn't Miss Lyster. It was Mrs. Meyer, a shawl thrown over her head and shoulders. He glanced past her. Mrs. Meyer was friendly enough, but she'd never before gone out of her way to talk to him. He waited for her to close the distance between them.

"Velcome back. I'm glad you are all right. Vhen your mule— Never mind. That is not vhy I come to see you. Jenny is out there." She waved a hand in the general direction of the street.

"She went to visit someone?" There were a few families living near Willow Creek. He'd noticed the wagon train was gone. No one to visit in that direction.

"Nein. She took a bucket and shovel and vent to get a plant."

"I see." He wasn't sure he understood. Did she expect him to go find her and help her dig out a plant? "I'm sure she'll be back soon."

"It is raining."

"It sure is." Hard, pounding, icy rain coming down

in sheets. "Why don't you go inside out of this weather? I'm done here. I'll take the wagon back."

"And then go find Jenny? She has been gone too long. She will be cold and vet."

"Very well. I'll go." Though he truly didn't see the need. She'd be on her way back. And by now she couldn't get any wetter. But he would go.

"Thank you." Mrs. Meyer hurried back to the house and seconds later appeared at the window, watching.

Finn hadn't been concerned, but Mrs. Meyer's anxiety was contagious. He quickly dumped the last few boards off the wagon then led the team over to Burnsie's corral, parked the wagon, and hurriedly took care of the animals.

Bill had followed and huddled at the back of the open-faced shed in the far corner.

Finn considered taking the mule with him but thought better of it. Bill hated rain and would balk the whole way, making Finn waste time.

Knowing Jenny would be wet and cold, he grabbed a blanket. He pulled his slicker collar higher around his neck and trotted down the muddy street. He reasoned she would have gone to the same place she had previously and kept up a brisk pace until he reached the spot. A slight depression showed where they'd dug out the buffalo bean, but other than that, nothing indicated she'd been there.

He climbed to the crest of the hill and looked around. He didn't see her. Now what? Had she gone a different direction? Was she, even now, back in the warm kitchen while he shivered in the rain?

He returned to the trail but didn't head toward town. Should he continue to look for her? Where? What would she be doing? Looking for flowers? Then she wouldn't likely be close to the trail. He looked around and, choosing the highest nearby hill, climbed three smaller ones to get to it and made his way to the top. The rain slackened off long enough for him to glimpse a patch of flowers. Maybe she'd gone there. He went that direction. A fresh hole gave him cause to think she'd dug out some flowers. But where was she? Had she gone back to the trail to make her way back to town while he climbed hills to get here? Had she gone farther? A different direction?

In this rain the hills all looked the same. Maybe she'd gotten turned around. Lost her way. Been discovered by someone or someones like that pair from the wagon train. In fact, how could he be certain they'd departed with the others?

Where was she?

He needed a plan. He looked around. He would climb to the top of each hill in each direction and if he didn't see anything, he'd give up. He set off at a trot, slipping several times in the wet grass.

At the top of the first hill, he stopped and carefully studied the view before him. Nothing out of the ordinary.

Slipping and sliding, he skidded down the hill and up the second one. He dashed the rain from his eyes so he could study his surroundings. Again, nothing to indicate Miss Lyster's presence. He hadn't been concerned when Mrs. Meyer asked him to find Miss Lyster. Even now, he told himself over and over, she was likely back in town, sitting before the fire in dry clothes, enjoying a cup of hot tea. But with every passing moment, his insides grew tenser. Why couldn't he find her? The rational part of him reminded him that it was a large country and she could have gone any direction. Like back to town. That's what any sensible person would do.

He'd climb one more hill.

And then he'd go back.

And if she wasn't there?

But she would be.

He reached the crest of the hill and again looked around. Again nothing. That was that. He'd done his best.

11

*J*enny opened her eyes. Why was she facedown on the ground? Why was she so cold and wet? Why did her head throb like someone pounded on it with her shovel?

Oh yes. She had gone out to find a plant. So why was she here? She lifted her head to look around. Rain slashed against her face. The world before her was shrouded in the fog of the falling rain, and it twisted and coiled in a most unusual way.

She moaned and closed her eyes against the nausea climbing up her throat.

The fog she'd glimpsed had seeped into her head, and her thoughts were wisps and fragments. How long had she been there? She was so cold. She couldn't stop shivering. Would it never stop raining?

One thought grew clear. She had to get home. Moaning and shivering, she tried to sit up. The nausea was so overwhelming, she retched and stayed on the ground. The cold, wet ground.

I must get up. I must get home.

She pushed herself up on her arms, sucked in damp air and held it, willing away the nausea. The world tipped sideways. Her arms folded and she again found herself flat on the ground.

Oh, God, help me. I can't stay here. Already the light was fading.

Again, she pushed herself up on her arms, pulled her knees under her, and rocked back and forth. She gritted her teeth against the persistent nausea and eased around until she sat on the ground. Her arms shaking, she wrapped them about her drawn-up legs, pressed her forehead to her knees, and breathed deeply in the hopes of calming her roiling insides and clearing her confused brain. It didn't help.

Shivering and moaning, so dizzy she couldn't tell if she tipped from side to side, she cried tears of frustration and fear. How long had she been here? How was she going to make it home when she couldn't even get to her feet?

Thudding. Like a large animal headed her direction.

Jenny tried to make her limbs move. Couldn't. Whatever animal approached, she was at its mercy. *Please, let it be quick and merciful.*

"Miss Lyster. I found you."

"Finn," she whispered without looking up.

"Are you hurt?"

"My head. Dizzy. Feel sick. Can't walk."

He sat beside her, his body anchoring her against the continual swaying. "You're freezing. Good thing I brought a blanket."

Fabric, warmed by his body and smelling like hay, covered her shoulders and was pulled tight across her front. His arms encircled her, and she leaned into his chest. She could smell oilskin, but her cheek didn't touch it. She tried to reason why. A slicker. Had he opened it to hold her against his warm chest? And her so wet?

She couldn't find the strength to protest.

Slowly, her body warmed though she was wet and clammy and very uncomfortable.

She lifted her head, squinting from one eye. "Is it dark out or is it just me?"

"It's dark."

"Oh." How long had she lain on the cold ground? "When did it start to rain?"

"Several hours ago. What happened to you?"

Slowly the memory and the words came. "It started to rain. I ran. Hoping to get home before I got soaked. I remember falling. Nothing else."

"You must have knocked yourself out."

"That would explain why my head hurts. And why I'm dizzy. How did you find me?"

He chuckled. The sound rumbled beneath her ear. Oh, what an awkward situation they were in. By rights, she should sit up, distance herself from him, but she couldn't make herself leave the warmth of his arms. And the idea of moving made her head spin.

"Your friend, Mrs. Meyer, asked me to find you and make sure you got home safely. You weren't easy to find."

"I was lost. Didn't know what direction to go." Her voice was small as she made the confession.

"Several times I wondered if you'd gone home and I was wandering around for no reason. But I just couldn't give up. I don't know why. It really didn't make any sense."

"Does to me. Glad you found me."

"Do you think you can stand?" He eased back.

She murmured a protest then silenced it. Rain and cold weren't going to kill her. They needed to get home. Her friends would be so worried. Besides, they had no choice. She couldn't stay here with a man. Imagine what the gossips would say. It would be exactly what Isaac would expect. She must get up. "I can walk."

He rose, leaving her shivering in the rain that had slowed to a fine mist, and held out his hands to help her.

Her limbs didn't get her message to stand. But he pulled her to her feet. Her knees folded. She forced them into a locked position. Her grip on his hands was all that kept her upright.

"Take a step."

The moment she lifted one leg to do so, the other gave out and she collapsed against him.

"I'll carry you."

She meant to protest but he swept her into his arms and began walking.

He stumbled. Stopped. Eased her to the ground. "I can't see well enough. I'm afraid I'll fall and injure you worse."

"But I need to get back to town." She pushed away from his steadying arms, swayed like a wind-battered sapling, and sank back against him. "I'll be all right in a minute."

One minute passed into another. And her strength did not return.

"We can't stay here all night." She heard the sharpness in her voice but couldn't help it.

"I don't think we have a choice. It's too dark to find our way safely, and you're too dizzy to walk."

"My parents would be shocked and shamed, and they don't need that with the way Isaac Stanley is acting." Too late she realized she'd said more than she should.

"First of all, I think your parents would be relieved to know you are safe."

"I hope so." But they were already dealing with the nastiness of gossip.

"And secondly, how are they to know? Are you going to write and tell them?"

"No. I guess I forgot how far away they are."

He shifted as if finding their position uncomfortable.

She tried to sit up, but he tightened his arms around her.

"Best you try and stay warm. Wouldn't want you to get pneumonia."

She did her best to relax against him, but her nerves twitched in protest. Their situation was most compromising.

"What did this Isaac Stanley say or do to upset your parents?"

"I can't rightly say." She felt him waiting for her to say more. "My mother wrote and said he was saying things about me that aren't true."

Finn tightened his arms around her. "He does not sound like a nice man."

"He's not, and yet I thought he was. I was foolish, wasn't I?" She didn't want to talk about that man any more. "Bill came back."

"I saw that."

"I think he wanted to be with Kent." She let that settle for a moment. "Bill likes little boys."

"Maybe I'll leave him behind when I go back to my cabin. He can keep both Kent and Eddie company."

"I hoped the trip to the fort would give you time to reconsider your decision."

"It gave me lots of time to think."

"And did you even give a thought to giving Eddie a home with you? The only person who has a connection to his mother and her family?"

"I gave it a great deal of thought. I simply don't think it's the best thing for him. If you won't give him a home, I'll ask one of the other ladies. Or see if Burnsie wants to raise him."

"Burnsie?" She sat up even though it left her head spinning. She could barely make out his features in the darkness. "He's old and lives in his store. What kind of life is that for a child?" She realized that it was the same argument Finn used to prove he couldn't keep the child and hoped he wouldn't notice.

"He'd have company. Kent and Sally across the street."

"That's not enough."

"Miss Lyster—"

"Oh please, if we are to spend the night together, at least call me Jenny."

He gulped audibly. "It's better than what I have."

He was stubborn and bullheaded and…so many things. She pulled the damp blanket around her clammy clothes and sat up, although she stayed very close to his side. She didn't want to be in his arms, resting on his chest, no matter how good it felt.

She would not talk anymore about Eddie. Not to someone who would not change his mind. "I wrote a letter to my parents and my brother," she said to indicate she was done with trying to make him see that he had lots to offer a child.

At almost the same time, he said, "I got the lumber and brought it back."

"Good to know," she said.

"I didn't know you had a brother."

"Ralph." Her smile gave a pleasant roundness to her

words. "He's six years older and always took such good care of me. I remember a time we went to a fair. I guess I was about six. So long ago. When I got tired, he put me on his shoulders and carried me. I sure do miss him."

"Where is he?"

"He went south and is working on a ranch in Wyoming Territory."

"Long ways from here."

"I haven't seen him in two years, and he isn't much of a letter writer." The rain had stopped, but clouds darkened the sky, making it impossible to see farther than her feet. "You've been to fairs, haven't you?"

"A few times. Mr. Moore showed his fine stallion, and I got to stay in the barn with him."

"You didn't get a chance to slip out and take in the sights?"

"After the Moores went home and I was left alone, I sneaked away to look around. Promise you won't tell Mr. Moore."

She chuckled, assuming he was joshing. "I think you are long past having to live up to Mr. Moore's orders."

"Yup. Up on the mountain I answer to no one."

She wanted to point out that he didn't need to answer to anyone in Willow Creek either, but she was tired of going over the same argument. "What did you see at the fair that you liked?"

"Cinnamon candy sticks. I never had any money but a friend of the Moores saw me drooling over them and bought me some. And the Ferris wheel fascinated me. I would have traded a hundred candy sticks for a ride."

"You never had one?"

"Not until I started working. Then I did. You ever ride one?"

"Ralph took me up several times." She tried to think what else they could talk about other than Ralph, because talking about him made her miss him too much. "Tell me about this Reverend Morgan you mentioned."

* * *

FINN HESITATED to answer her question. The past two days, his mind had been flooded with a kaleidoscope of memories. Many that he'd tried to bury. Didn't want to remember. But also some he was glad to recall. "Reverend Morgan seemed to make a point of seeking out a poor, lonely orphan boy. I don't know that Mr. Moore approved, but he could hardly say anything. The reverend would sit beside me. Didn't matter if it was in the barn or out at the woodpile and read to me from the Bible. I didn't understand a lot of it, but I liked listening to him and he always explained what he read."

"That sounds nice. Like someone cared about you."

"Yup. Though Mr. Moore cared so long as I did the work he gave me."

"That's not the same."

Which, he might point out, is why he couldn't take Eddie. Work was all he knew. Another memory came, unbidden and unwelcome. "Once Ethel came to the barn at the fair and asked me to show her around."

Jenny jerked about to face him though the darkness of the sky made it impossible to see more than each other's shapes. "What? How old were you?"

"We were probably close to fourteen." Suddenly the words could not be held back. "She was so friendly that it gave me courage to think she cared. That's when I began to seek her out. Later, when she said I had nothing to offer her, I asked about that day. She said she was only defying her father, who had forbidden her to go without him at her side."

"Oh, Finn, that's so cruel. And yet—"

He cut her off, certain she was going to bring up Eddie again. "I should have known her attention meant nothing."

"Do you hear from your friend, the Reverend Morgan?"

His friend? He'd never thought of the older man's attention that way. "He writes from time to time. Doesn't even wait for me to write back."

"That's nice."

Another memory jolted through him. "He was a friend of my parents. I forgot that." He knew he likely sounded as surprised as he felt. But how could he forget that sole connection to his parents? "I remember him coming to visit at our home. He always spoke to me, asked what I was doing. I recall one occasion when I was attempting to build a miniature barn for the farm animals my father carved for me. Pa was giving me instructions. Reverend Morgan looked at it and said I was a very talented boy. I'd forgotten that, too."

"Finn, how special. So you were a loved and cherished child."

His throat threatened to close off with his sense of loss. "I wish I hadn't remembered."

"Why?" She touched his arm. "To know you were loved must make you feel good."

Even through his slicker he felt the coolness of her fingers. "You must be cold. I wish I could start a fire, but everything is soaking wet."

"I'm all right. And I'm not going to let you change the subject. You said you didn't remember your parents, and yet here you have a very special memory. I think you remember a lot more than you realize or acknowledge. Finn, why don't you want to remember a home that appears to have been loving and kind?"

"Because it's gone." Every word scraped up his throat and across his tongue. There was nothing left of that boy who was loved. Now he was a man who had grown up believing he had to work to survive. No time or room or care for anything but his work.

"You're not gone. You are the boy born of your parents, loved by your parents. A boy who was instructed kindly and taught pleasurable activities. Something besides work."

He leaned over his knees at her words that attacked

everything he believed about himself. Everything he'd learned to believe because of Mr. Moore's insistence.

"Finn." Her fingers tightened on his arm. "You were an orphan boy. But you don't have to remain one. You can choose to be Finn Johnson—the boy you were born to be. The man you were born to be."

"How can I be something that is dead?"

"Your memories aren't dead. Neither is the boy you were. There's a verse in the Bible. I'm not sure I can remember it correctly, but it says something about God knowing you and forming you before you were born." She paused, either to let him think about what she said or to consider what she would say next.

Could he hope she was done?

She continued. "He knew you, made you, and He has great plans for you."

He didn't reply, because he knew to take the discussion any further would be to invite her to say she believed God's plans meant he should give Eddie a home. He still firmly believed the best, kindest thing for Eddie was a home with people far better equipped to bring him up properly.

Like his parents would have brought Finn up if they had lived.

"Why was I allowed to survive?" Had he just spoken those self-pitying words aloud? "Forget I said that. It isn't what I meant. It came out wrong." He clamped his mouth shut and wished for enough light to go back to Willow Creek.

12

Jenny knew that Finn had spoken from his heart, revealing a truth that startled him and seemed to frighten him as well. "Finn, I believe your parents would be glad you lived." No sign that he'd heard, though she knew he couldn't help but hear. "Were you with them when they had their accident?"

He shrugged.

But of course he knew.

She asked a few more questions, but he gave one syllable answers. Finally, she admitted defeat. Her head still hurt. Her stomach lurched if she moved too fast. It had been a very long day that had extended into the night.

She didn't have enough energy to think what the morning would bring. She shifted so she could rest her head on her knees.

. . .

Jenny wakened to someone shaking her bed. Her hard, cold bed. And why did her head hurt so badly, like her own private thunderstorm between her ears?

"Jenny, wake up. It's light enough to make our way to town."

She sat up and groaned at the way her head protested the sudden movement. Oh, no. It wasn't a bad dream. She had spent the night alone with Finn out in the hills. Her clothes were wet. She was chilled to the bone.

"Jenny...Miss Lyster...are you fit for walking?" He hovered above her in the faint gray light that indicated dawn would soon be upon them.

"I can walk." She took his offered hand and forced her stiff limbs to stand, clamping down on the groan rushing up her throat, followed by a wave of nausea. "I can do this." She took a stumbling step forward and another. Each one a test of her ability to stay upright. "How far is it?"

"It's a ways. Can't rightly say how far as I wandered around trying to locate you. Let me carry you."

She shook her head. "I can manage." She would not give in to weakness. "Did I ever thank you? If not, I'm doing it now." The words coming through gritted teeth didn't sound grateful, but at the moment all she cared about was staying on her feet.

"Hang on to my arm." He crooked his elbow toward her.

She looked at him then, seeing him clearly for the first time since he'd found her. Her eyes widened. "You got your hair cut and your beard trimmed." She closed one eye so she could focus better. "It looks nice."

"Thank you."

She took his waiting arm and they began the journey back to town. Every step taxed her strength, but she had no choice but to continue onward.

"There's the trail." Finn's words snapped her from her single-minded concentration on placing one foot in front of the other. "Can you keep going?"

"Do I have a choice?"

"You could wait here while I go get a wagon."

She looked each way down the trail and shuddered. "I want to go home."

"Very well. But if you change your mind, you let me know."

"I am not a quitter," she muttered. "I can do hard things. People ought to take me seriously." More than a pretty face, she added to herself, though she wondered if anyone would accuse her of that at the moment. She must be a sight.

"You are no quitter, and you are a force to be dealt with. You're strong and courageous."

"I most certainly am." She muttered the same words over and over as they walked along the muddy trail. "Only I don't feel very strong right now..." Weakness she couldn't control rushed through her body and she swayed.

Finn grabbed her. "Sit down for a minute."

She didn't seem to have much choice. She sank to the ground, leaning forward over her knees and willing away the faintness.

Finn sat facing her. "Will you let me carry you?"

She shook her head, felt his concern, perhaps his impatience, but couldn't look at him. Couldn't bear to see his disappointment. "I'm sorry," she mumbled. "Go ahead without me."

"I'll give you a minute or two to recover."

"I'm sorry for being weak and useless." And sorry for the whining note in her voice.

He chuckled. "Who says you're weak and useless? Not me."

She turned her face to look at him. "Only because you're too kind."

"Something I've never been accused of before." He dipped his head to look into her eyes more closely. "You're doing just fine, considering the size of the lump on your forehead."

She touched it and winced. "Good thing I've got a rock-hard head."

"Do you?"

She couldn't turn away from his probing look. "I must have."

"Then why do you let unkind comments bother you so much?"

She sat up, the sudden movement making the world spin. "Aren't we right back to where we started? I could ask you the same thing." Only now, having tried to make him see how foolish it was to do so, she felt a twinge of truth in his words. Was she letting how the Stanleys treated her and the words they spoke about her have more weight than they should? Had she overreacted? Acted hastily? "You might be right, though. I let their words and actions wound me more deeply than I should have. It's just..." How did she explain why she had? "So much of my life I was judged unfairly because of my looks. If I won a contest at school, the girls said it was because of my looks. If I came in last, someone would say it didn't matter because I could use my looks to get what I wanted. Brash boys seemed to think I would welcome their awkward advances. The nice boys shied away from me as if something about me scared them. These." She jabbed at her eyes. "Why couldn't I have plain brown eyes like my brother?"

"So you think your most beautiful feature is—"

"Like I said, a curse."

"Have you ever considered that people are startled at your unusual eyes but attracted by you kind and generous spirit?"

She held his gaze for a long time, seeking truth and more, though she wasn't sure what the more was. Acceptance? Validation? A smile began in a secret corner of her heart and burned a trail through her insides right to her mouth. "Finn, I am almost persuaded to believe you."

"You *should* believe me."

She sat up so she could see him better. "I'll tell you what. I'll believe you if you believe me."

He didn't ask what she meant, because he obviously knew. Instead, he turned toward the trail. "We are about to be rescued. Stay here while I meet the wagon." He was on his feet, waiting for the approaching travelers.

Jenny watched him. If they'd had a few more minutes, she might have convinced him he was a man with more to offer the world than his back as he went up the mountain or as he bent over a task. Work or retreat. *Finn, you deserve so much more.*

And once he believed it, he would be ready to give Eddie a home.

FINN COULDN'T SAY if he was glad or disappointed to see the approaching wagon. He had almost made Jenny see that she didn't need to believe what the Stanleys had said or put too much stock in how others had treated her. Anyone who got to know her saw her true worth. Her friends certainly did.

He didn't want to argue about his own beliefs, although he was beginning to see that he was more than an orphan boy. Remembering his parents and having Jenny point out how much he was loved had pushed him close to believing. He was no coward, but the idea of changing who and what he thought he was had him quaking inside.

Thankfully, the approaching wagon provided the perfect excuse for abandoning both the conversation and the mental wranglings. He stood at the side of the road, waiting. In a few minutes he recognized the occupants of the wagon and waved his hat.

Blaze and his wife drew abreast. "Finn, what are you doing here?" Blaze's gaze went past Finn, and his eyes widened. "Isn't that Miss Lyster from the bakery?"

"It is. She fell and hurt her head and can't make it back to town. I'm hoping you'll give us a ride."

"By all means." He set the brake and secured the reins.

His wife stood. "Help me down, dear." The woman was heavy with child.

Blaze lifted her to the ground. She picked up her skirts and hurried over to Jenny—Miss Lyster—Finn would have to remember to call her that and not Jenny as he'd been thinking of her these past hours.

Mrs. Hooper bent over Jenny. "My dear, what happened?"

"Bumped my head." Jenny touched her forehead and winced.

"Your clothes are wet." Mrs. Hooper pressed her hand to Jenny's arm. "And you're cold as ice. Blaze." She turned to her husband. "We need to get her to town quickly."

Blaze went to Jenny's side, Finn on his heels. They half lifted Jenny to her feet and across the muddy ruts to the wagon and helped her into the back. She scuttled to the sideboards and sat pressed against them. Her face colorless except for the redness of the bruise.

Finn jumped into the wagon and sat opposite her.

"Thank you, everyone," she murmured, then buried her head to her knees.

Blaze and his wife stood at the back, looking from Jenny to Finn and then at each other. Finn knew their looks carried questions about how long had he and Jenny been out together. Alone. Unchaperoned. The truth could not be hidden. It could only be dealt with.

The Hoopers returned to the bench and the wagon jarred into motion. Jenny's knuckles whitened at each bounce. If not for so many things, including what Blaze and his wife would think and how Jenny would resist, Finn would sit at her side and hold her tight, softening the ride as best he could.

What were her friends going to say? The question hammered at his head. He'd know soon enough as they passed a tree that grew close to the trail a mile from town.

Mr. Moore's voice echoed in his head. *An orphan boy should be seen and not heard. Be grateful for a home. Do your work cheerfully.*

He blinked. He could barely hear the words. Instead, Jenny's voice almost drowned them out. He was more than an orphan boy. He had been loved. He was free to be…do… He couldn't find the words, but for the first time, he wondered if his future offered something better.

They passed the livery and blacksmith. They passed the harness shop on which a Closed sign hung. Burnsie's store was opposite and then they were at the café and bakery. The wagon stopped. Jenny's friends stood in front of the establishment. Several people gathered there. Others ran down the street to join them. Had the whole town been alerted to their absence? It looked like many of the townspeople were preparing to go searching for them. This did not bode well for him. He knew how ready people were to judge. The best thing he could do for both their sakes was find Bill and make his way back to his mountain cabin.

Finn waited until Blaze helped Jenny down into the waiting arms of her friends and people crowded around them, asking what had happened and wanting to know if she was all right.

Then he slipped from the wagon, hoping he could steal away.

Bill whinnied a greeting. Great. So much for not being noticed.

Burnsie and the blacksmith looked up at the mule's noise then crossed to him.

"You found her last night?" Burnsie asked.

"She'd been knocked out." Shouldn't that be excuse enough?

The others crowded around him.

"You spent the night with her?" one asked.

He saw no need to answer. They knew the facts and had drawn their own conclusions.

"Her reputation must be protected." "It isn't proper." "You'll have to marry her." "She will be marked as having poor morals." The voices barreled at him.

He would have walked away, left town, left these

narrow-minded people to their own amusement, except for that last statement. He could not be responsible for doing anything to make Jenny think others regarded her the same way the Stanleys did.

"No doubt Miss Lyster has something to say about this," he said. "But shouldn't your first concern be to get her warmed up and tend to that bump on her head?" As he hoped, they looked sheepish.

Meanwhile, her friends had taken her indoors.

The blacksmith stood before Finn, his legs wide, his massive arms crossed over his chest. "This is not done with."

Finn nodded. "Didn't think it was." He touched the brim of his hat in a farewell salute and sauntered to his campsite, Bill at his heels. He built a fire, made coffee, and hunkered down to think.

He'd marry her if she'd have him. Anything to protect her. Besides, it would provide the perfect solution for Eddie. If she'd agree to what he had in mind.

But he wouldn't marry her just because others insisted.

JENNY ACCEPTED the ministrations of her friends. They helped her out of her clammy, clinging clothes and into dry ones. They sat her beside the hot stove with a blanket around her shoulders. Hilda examined her bruise then dabbed at it, making soothing sounds as she applied some sort of ointment.

Slowly, warmth returned to Jenny's body. The hot coffee Laura handed her helped to clear her brain. She grew aware that the others hovered close by watching, waiting.

"What?" she asked.

"Vell, first, ve are glad you are safe and sound."

"Thank you."

Laura cleared her throat. "We were worried. Everyone had gathered to go searching for you when you showed up."

"I was safe."

"But not alone. Which is a mixed blessing."

She heard the sad, warning note in Laura's voice and sat up straighter, the blanket falling from her shoulders. "What do you mean?"

Laura wouldn't answer. Hilda shook her head sadly.

"You spent the night alone with a man," Delcie said.

"I had to. It was dark. I was dizzy. I couldn't even walk." The words sputtered forth.

"But now you must do what is right and proper."

Delcie spoke, but a glance at the others and Jenny knew they all agreed.

"What are you saying?" She knew, but she would make them spell it out.

"You and he vill have to marry." At least Hilda sounded regretful.

"What if we don't want to? We don't love each other." She stared from one to the other, shock clouding her brain. "I hardly know the man." Though there was something about him that created a tenuous connection. Perhaps because they had both felt the sting of open criticism. And their unfortunate night in the hills opened them up to more of the same.

Delcie crossed her arms. "What kind of example are you setting for the children if you don't? Will they grow up thinking there are no consequences for what we do?" The children could be heard playing in the bedroom where they would not be able to overhear this conversation.

Jenny's throat tightened. She did not want to marry a man who didn't love her. But if she didn't, was she going to live with the shadow of last night hanging over her? A weight to match that of how the Stanleys had treated her. "He's a mountain man. I expect he'll retreat to his cabin." The only reason he was still here was to wait for Eddie.

"You mean he would have no regard for your reputation?" Laura's softly spoken words conveyed enough shock and surprise to make Jenny realize how seriously she was taking this whole situation.

"People will soon forget." Everyone but her, perhaps.

"People do not forget, ever." Delcie said.

Hilda clapped her hands to her knees. "Ve vill have to speak to Finn." She rose. "Come ladies. Jenny, you vill watch the children."

The three of them exited like a train under full steam.

Jenny leaned back. How had she managed to get

herself into such a predicament? Not through any carelessness of her own. At least it wasn't because her eyes had bewitched some man, as Mr. Stanley had suggested. It was too dark for that.

But being forced to marry? True, she didn't hold out for romance and love. Perhaps a marriage to Finn would mean no man would again feel he could take advantage of her. She hadn't told Finn, because she was loath to talk about it, but Mr. Stanley wasn't the first one to be inappropriate, just the most aggressive. But she couldn't see Finn agreeing to a marriage. Like she said, he and Bill would simply leave.

She could, too. But where would she go? Could she join Ralph? But would things really be any different wherever she went? And how many times could she uproot her life and leave friends behind?

She was too weary to think about it right now.

Her friends returned but she didn't give them a chance to repeat what had been said. "I'm too tired to think." She quickly withdrew to her bed and fell asleep in minutes.

SHE WAKENED to the murmur of voices in the kitchen and lay motionless, trying to hear what was said. Hilda's voice was the only one she could make out.

"Dey vill realize dey must do this." Hilda's accent had deepened, making it clear how upset she was.

Jenny knew Hilda meant her. She and Finn. They were talking about them needing to marry. She rose and joined them, ignoring the lingering dizziness. At least it had lessened enough she could walk under her own steam. "Are you serious about this?" She glanced from one to the other. Hilda's smile was sorrowful. Delcie's eyes challenging.

"You need to talk to Finn," Laura said. She pointed out the window.

Jenny looked out and saw Finn patting soil around a plant where she meant to put the buffalo bean she'd dug up. "He went and got the bucket and shovel? How long have I been sleeping?" Beyond where he worked stood a section of completed fence. She had slept through the pounding of him hammering.

"It's midafternoon. Laura wanted to waken you and make sure you were all right, but Hilda wouldn't let her."

She didn't wait for Delcie to finish before she grabbed the doorknob and stepped outside.

Finn heard her and rose to his full height, dusting his hands on his trousers. "How are you feeling?"

"Fine. And you?"

"Fine as well."

"You got my plant. Thank you." She didn't know what else to say though it seemed there was so much they needed to discuss.

"Why don't we go for a walk away from curious eyes?" he said.

Her friends watched from the window. He tipped his head toward the street where Bill watched. "At least he won't judge us for what we say or do."

She fell into step beside him and they sauntered toward the river. She was certain dozens of eyes followed their every move. "I'm sorry to have sucked you into this."

"It's no more your fault than mine. We've done nothing wrong, so I refuse to feel guilty."

"I wish everyone could see we are innocent." They stopped at the edge of the trees. Far enough from town that their conversation couldn't be overheard, yet still visible so all those judging eyes could see they weren't guilty of anything. Except being stranded overnight.

She spoke first. "I don't know what my friends said, but they do not speak for me."

"But they do represent what everyone is thinking."

"Does that matter to you?"

He shrugged. "Not a great deal. But it is something you will have to live with the rest of your life. And there are those who would judge you wrongly for it."

"You mean even more than they judge me for these eyes?"

"More fuel for the fire of their faulty conclusions."

At least he'd made it sound like they were wrong, and he didn't agree with them. "Why must people be so small-minded? So critical and hurtful?"

"Miss Lyster—"

"Jenny, please, at least when we are alone."

"Jenny, I am not opposed to marrying you."

The ground could have opened up and swallowed

her and she wouldn't have been any more surprised. "What did you say?"

"I'll marry you if you are agreeable."

"Why?"

"Is it so hard to think of marrying me?"

She heard the pain in his voice. "Oh, Finn, it isn't because you aren't a good man. You are. But don't you want to marry someone who loves you?" As soon as she spoke, she knew he didn't expect love from anyone. Her heart ached for him. "You deserve that."

"So do you."

"Maybe I don't want it." Yet speaking those words sent her insides into a frenzied housefly dance of protest. She quickly quelled the turmoil.

He continued. "Then hear me out. We could agree to marriage. No expectations on either of us. Between us, we could give Eddie a home."

"Between us? What do you mean?"

"He'd have two people to care for him. He'd have a home." He waited, letting her think through his offer.

"You'd give up your home on the mountain?"

His gaze held hers steadily. "I don't think that would be necessary. Marriage wouldn't change who I am. What I propose is we marry. Neither of us expects or wants a wild, flaming romance. You and Eddie stay here. You could continue to live where you are, or I could build you a house."

"We wouldn't even live together?" Shock made her voice shrill.

Bill, who had followed them, lifted his head and snorted.

Finn's ruddy face darkened. "I didn't think you would want it."

She curled and uncurled her fingers. "I don't know what I want."

"I don't think we should be bullied into marrying before sundown."

"Did someone suggest it?"

"The smithy is pretty set on seeing things done the right way."

Jenny chuckled at the droll tone of Finn's voice. "By that, he means his way?"

"Exactly. Why don't we tell them we need a while to make plans, and then they'll leave us alone? It will give you time to think what you want to do."

Her mind whirled until the dizziness she'd thought she'd overcome returned. If they married, she would be mother to a child. Eddie would not feel rejected by Finn. Basically, they could continue as they were with a few minor adjustments.

"I don't need time to make a decision. Finn, I will agree to marry you on one condition."

13

"*Y*ou do? You will?" Finn stumbled on the words. He hadn't expected her to agree so easily. Then he remembered there had been more. "What condition?"

"We get to know each other better before we marry."

He turned his gaze toward the mountains. "There isn't much to know about me. You already know that I was orphaned at a young age and was foolish enough to think Ethel's kindness meant more than it did."

"Yes. I also know you don't think you deserve to have the sort of life you had with your parents and that nothing matters about you but your work. But I don't know what your favorite color is, what you like to eat, what sort of things you enjoy doing apart from work."

He slowly brought his gaze to her.

She met his look, hers open and inviting.

"I like blue. Like the summer sky. I eat anything—"

"Would you prefer chocolate cake or ginger cookies?"

"Yes."

She laughed. "Hilda says the Mountie is out on patrol and won't be back for a week, maybe two. He's the only one who has authority to marry us. Can we use that time to get to know more about each other?"

He knew they could go to Fort Macleod and get married but he liked her suggestion. "It's a delay even the smithy will accept, so yes, I agree to that."

"Great. Now what?"

"I have no idea." He'd never courted a woman though this wasn't exactly a courting situation. He didn't know what it was nor what she expected. Hopefully she would tell him or in some way make it clear.

"I suppose we should let people know."

He chuckled at the way her voice deepened, revealing how little she cared to do so. "We can at least put your friends' concern to rest." They had been very clear about what they expected to happen.

"By the way, what did my friends say to you?"

"Mrs. Meyers said your reputation must be protected. Miss Fisher could not bring herself to look at me, while Miss Morton's gaze practically drilled holes through me."

She grinned and her eyes flashed with the afternoon sun. "There you have them in a nutshell. Hilda, practical. Let's get things done. Laura, anxious and cautious to a fault, and Delcie so defensive."

"And you?"

She sobered, her head tipped to one side. "Yes, me. How do you see me in one or two words?"

Heat threatened to suffocate him. He had no desire to make a personal comment. One that might offend. Was this part of getting to know each other better? One word? Two? His mind stalled. Refused to work.

"Finn, I'm waiting." Her tone was half teasing, half pleading.

"Kind. I'd say you are kind." He managed to get the words past his tight throat without choking on them.

"That's nice. I like that."

Was she going to give a word to describe him? If only he dared ask.

She grinned. "I see you're waiting for me to say something about you." She tipped her head from side to side and studied him long enough to make his skin tighten.

"Finn, I can't find one word. Besides, I already told you how I view you. Except—" She paused, made him wait, his breath stuck halfway up his throat. "Lonely. I see you as lonely."

He shook his head, prepared to deny it, but no words came.

She patted his arm. "But that is about to change. You'll soon be a family man with me for your wife and Eddie for your son."

"I'm not lonely just because I'm alone." Words burst

forth in a torrent. "I'm alone because…" He had no way to describe it. "Because I prefer it. Better than being treated as invisible. Better than…"

"Being valued only for your work. But not everyone is like Mr. Moore. Some respect you for who you are as well as what you do. They see a man who does what is honorable, goes out of his way not to hurt others, and keeps his word."

His jaw fell slack. He made himself click it closed. She had drawn those conclusions based on what? He struggled to fight against how they touched him, yet he couldn't deny the feeling that they struck a chord deep in the core of his being.

"You are too kind." He tried for a droll tone but wondered if he succeeded.

"Come on, let's go tell them." She tucked her hand into the crook of his arm.

And something inside him softened at the gesture.

Before they reached the café, the smithy saw them and headed their direction. Burnsie crossed the street, all of them aiming for the front door of the eating establishment.

Mrs. Meyer opened the door at their approach.

"Seems we were being watched closely," Jenny murmured. "Isn't it nice to know everyone is so concerned for us?"

He didn't miss the sarcasm in her voice and grinned. "Maybe a little too nice?"

They had reached the door, making it impossible for either of them to say anything more to each other without being overheard, but she squeezed his arm and he knew they were united in their opinion.

Neither of them would have chosen this route except for the pressure from others. And his desire to do what was right by her.

They stood side by side, her hand still on his arm, firm and warm.

He dropped his hat on the nearest table and faced the others. Like an accused man before a jury. A guilty man. He would take his sentence along with Jenny. But at least she had willingly agreed to the judgment forced upon them.

"We have come to a decision," she said.

He would not let her be the sole bearer of their news. "We will marry and satisfy the demands of our society, but the Mountie is away, so we must wait until he returns."

"Until then," the smithy said, in his deep, rumbling voice. "You will not be together."

Jenny's fingers dug into his arm. They had not seen this coming.

"Until then," Finn said, with a firmness that surprised him, "Jenny and I have decided we will use the time to get to know one another better." He knew he wore a stubborn expression. It felt strange compared to his yes-sir usual demeanor. But this wasn't about him. It was about Jenny.

The smithy sputtered.

Mrs. Meyer held up her hand to forestall any disagreement. "That is a fine idea."

No one offered an argument though Finn thought the smithy looked about ready to explode.

"Now shouldn't ve all get back to our vork." Mrs. Meyer made shooing motions, and the men tramped out the door.

The other ladies returned to the kitchen until only Mrs. Meyer faced them. "You have chosen visely. You vill have decisions to make as you plan a future together." With that she left the room.

The air left Jenny's lungs in a whoosh. Did she wobble? What was wrong with him? Had he forgotten about the knock on her head? The bruise that still discolored her skin?

"You better sit down." He guided her to a chair.

Mrs. Meyer must have been watching for she hustled over with two cups of coffee and a plate of cookies. "You two talk."

Finn barely got "Thanks," out before she scuttled away.

"I don't know what she thinks we need to decide." Jenny sounded both weary and confused.

"Who knows what she thinks? All that matters is what we think."

Jenny's head came up. Her eyes flashed and a smile slowly crept to her mouth. "Thank you. I was getting all knotted up inside." She touched her forehead. "Like this."

"Are you sure you're all right? That's a nasty looking bruise." He lifted his hand, then thought better of touching her. But if they were to be man and wife, even if only on paper...he brushed his fingers across the bruise. "Does it hurt very much?"

Her gaze clung to his. "No. I'm fine."

For being fine, her voice seemed strained. Was it because he had touched her? He slowly pulled his hand back.

The aroma of a meal cooking made his stomach growl, and she chuckled softly. "I think it's almost suppertime. I should be helping." She made it as far as the kitchen before Mrs. Meyer waved her away.

"You get to know that young man."

Jenny returned. "What do we do?"

Through the window overlooking the street, he watched four men approach. "Let's get out of here." He rose and grabbed her hand and headed for the kitchen.

She held back. "What about supper?"

"You go out back." Mrs. Meyer shooed them away. "You can eat after the customers have come and gone."

Finn didn't look at the other ladies. Would they resent that he was taking Jenny from the work?

"Go," Mrs. Meyer said. "Ah. Finn, I see you are vorried about the vork. No need. Ve can manage. Go. Go."

Grinning, Finn led Jenny out the back door, across the yard, and around the corner of the shed, out of sight of the street.

"That's a first." Her voice grew bubbly and then another soft chuckle emerged. Her eyes sparkled.

He couldn't stop staring at her even though he knew he ought to turn away. But why? They were to be married. Didn't that give him the right to openly admire her? Within reason?

Her laughter ended. Her smile faded. But her eyes continued to hold his. "Finn?"

"What?"

"I think it might be fun getting to know you better."

A whole world of expectations. "I hope you feel the same when the Mountie returns."

What if she decided she didn't want to marry him? Not even a marriage in name only?

She caught his sleeve. "Let's sit here and enjoy the quiet." She lowered herself to the ground, drawing him down with her.

They sat side by side. He might as well enjoy the moment and deal with the future when the future arrived.

* * *

JENNY LEANED her head back against the shed. Her shoulder pressed into Finn's. She left her hand on his arm, liking the strength she felt beneath the fabric of his shirt. He had defended her. Was prepared to marry her to protect her reputation. What a stark contrast to how Isaac had been. It was a breath of clean, refreshing air to her heart. She wished she had a way to make Finn understand how grateful she was. Words would have to do.

"Thank you for looking for me last night. For

finding me and staying with me. Protecting me." Her throat thickened as she recalled how afraid and alone she'd been when she wakened to discover herself lost in the dark. "Thank you for caring about my reputation."

"Of course I do. I always try and do what's right."

Those last words didn't sit well with Jenny. "For others but not for yourself." She shifted so she could face him. "Finn, I can't marry you if it's not the right thing for you."

He studied her. She sensed his surprise followed quickly by caution and then a slow smile.

"Jenny Lyster, you are the first person who's ever considered my feelings."

The words ached through her then she realized they weren't true. "Except for your parents and Reverend Morgan."

"You're right. How could I overlook that?"

"I think because you have spent most of your life telling yourself that lie."

He stared at her, his eyes wide, his lips parted as if he couldn't get in a breath. Then he shifted his gaze away, past her to some place distant in his mind.

She waited, wondering if he was offended at her comment but, knowing it to be true, she wouldn't withdraw it.

His gaze returned to hers, a look of both surprise and regret on his face. "You're more right than you know. I realize I spent most of my growing up years trying to please someone. Then the next eight years proving I didn't need or want anyone or their approval."

She nodded, hoping he would say more.

"In the end, I pleased no one."

"Maybe it's time to stop thinking about others and do what is right and good for you according to God's word." *Please, Lord, help me remember a verse that would help him understand.* She couldn't be sure the words that came to mind were from the Bible or something she'd heard at one time. "I think there's a Bible verse that says the Lord rejoices over us with joy."

"That's in the Bible?"

"I think so. Isn't it a nice thought?"

"You're sure it's in the Bible?"

"I wish I could be certain, but I'm not. I'll see if I can find it."

He jolted like something had struck him. "It's Saturday, isn't it?"

"I believe so." Which would be why so many people had been in the street. No doubt all of them hearing about Jenny and Finn spending the night together.

"I have an idea. Do you have to work tomorrow?"

"Hilda closes the café on Sunday. Says we all need a day of rest."

"Then how would you like to go to a special church service?"

"Here?" She and the other women had been attending the services in the nearby church since their arrival. The preacher came out from Fort Macleod. He could marry them. Why hadn't she thought of that?

But waiting for the Mountie provided the space they needed to learn about each other, so she didn't mention it.

"No. I have something else in mind. The Hooper ranch. They don't often come into town but instead have their own Sunday service at the ranch. I've been once and it was very good. Would you like to go?"

"You mean we'd be away from all those accusing eyes? Yes, of course, I'd like to go."

He laughed at her enthusiasm. "We'll have to leave early. I think they meet shortly after breakfast."

"Tell me the time and I'll be ready."

Hilda came around the corner of the shed with two plates of food. "Thought you two might be getting hungry."

Jenny half pushed to her feet. "I should be helping."

Hilda waved her away. "No need. Ve can manage just fine for a day or two. Enjoy your time together." She returned to the kitchen.

Jenny stared after her. "I feel guilty."

Finn touched the back of her hand. "You don't need to prove anything, you know."

She met his gaze. "Is that what I'm trying to do?"

"Aren't you? Wanting people to see you as useful?"

Her grin was self-mocking. "Maybe you know too much about me already."

His eyes crinkled at the corners. "Does that mean you want to go to the fort and get married right away?"

She sputtered a protest that ended in a laugh. "Let's stick to our original plan."

"Good idea."

They both bent to their food, and conversation ended for a few minutes. Then a thought hit her. "The Hoopers won't mind us inviting ourselves to their service?"

"Nope. They said for me to drop in anytime."

"You? What about me?"

He leaned forward, his nose very close to hers. "And why would they object? They already have four beautiful young women in their midst. One more will be as welcome as a new flower blooming next to the house."

"Finn, you're a poet."

His complexion darkened.

She held his gaze. "Finn, I do, indeed, believe I'm going to enjoy getting to know you better—the poet, the woodsman, the...everything." Heat crept up her neck and pooled in her cheeks.

His gaze went past her, and he laughed. "Don't be surprised if a cold nose is pressed to your neck."

She turned around and held up her hand to Bill. "No cold nose."

Bill snuffled and turned away as if he was innocent of any such idea.

She laughed. "Your mule has an attitude. I expect he keeps you amused."

"Or annoyed."

His droll tone tickled her insides. "A poet with a

sense of humor. Getting to know you could prove very entertaining." She quite looked forward to it.

Never mind that he looked ready to bolt to his feet and drag his mule up the mountain. He just might enjoy learning to loosen up.

14

Finn had a restless night as thoughts tossed about in his mind. Jenny had agreed to marry him. Wanted to get to know him better. Thought God would rejoice over him. He'd unsuccessfully searched for those words in the Bible but had given up as darkness closed in around him. It was a nice thought but perhaps not God's words.

His mind bounced from regret at having asked Jenny to go with him to the Coulee Crossing Ranch to anticipating it so much he counted the hours until morning.

Dawn was still a distant promise when he rolled from his bed. He built a fire to make coffee, fed and watered Bill, then downed the coffee and half a loaf of bread he'd bought at the bakery. Jenny said she sometimes made the bread though it was Hilda who made most of it. Because Jenny had been busy with other things yesterday he assumed Hilda had made this loaf. The idea of entering a house to be greeted by the smell of fresh bread, the smile of a woman, and the laughter of a child...

No time for daydreaming this morning. He'd arranged for a wagon at the livery and hurried to get it then drove the few yards to the bakery. Jenny stepped out as he drew to a halt.

"Good morning," she said, a smile widening her mouth and rounding her words. Her eyes flashed what he hoped was anticipation. She wore a bonnet of dark forest green that made her eyes appear darker than usual. A matching cape covered her shoulders against the morning cool. Her dress was some sort of soft-looking material in brownish gold, the color of autumn leaves. It might have appeared dull on another woman but on her, it glowed.

"Morning to you too." He had found a private spot in the creek where he could bathe and had gone there earlier in the morning. He'd put on a decent shirt and brushed his buckskin vest so it looked its best. He'd even cleaned his boots.

He jumped down and took her hand to help her up.

"Thank you," she said, and leaned closer to whisper, "I feel like everyone has heard what we're doing. I think there are a pair of eyes in every window."

He glanced past her to the store. Sure enough, Burnsie watched. Didn't even bother drawing back when he saw Finn had seen him.

Finn grinned up at Jenny. "Don't suppose they have

anything more interesting to do." He went around, got up beside her, and flicked the reins.

"You don't resent the way people are fussing about our business?"

"Would they stop if I did?"

"I doubt it."

"Then I choose to ignore it."

"Finn, you should apply that philosophy to the things Mr. Moore said, too."

"Maybe I will." For the first time he didn't care what the man had said. Today was his and Jenny's and he didn't intend to let his former boss…and owner… ruin it.

She chuckled. "Good to know."

They were soon out of town and rolling along the trail toward the ranch.

"Have you meet the Hoopers?" he asked.

"Audrey has been to visit twice, but I guess she's not a Hooper anymore."

"Once a Hooper, always a Hooper."

She laughed as he had hoped she would. "Blaze and Emma rescued us from our little adventure." She batted her eyes at him, and he chuckled. "The others came by to welcome us shortly after we arrived. Not all at once." She jerked around to look directly at him, her eyes wide and dark. "I've never met them all at once. There'd be…" She ticked off her fingers as she counted up each member of the Hooper family. "Ten… no, eleven."

"Thirteen with us."

She settled back, staring straight ahead and worrying her fingers.

Why did this fact have her so flustered? "There'd be more than that if we attended church in Willow Creek."

"But this is just family. Eleven of them. I grew up with one brother who was considerably older. I can't imagine such a large family."

"Four brothers and one sister. They take care of each other." His voice deepened. "I think it would be nice to have had brothers or sisters."

She patted his arm. "I think what you needed and wanted was to feel like you belonged in a family."

"You could be right." He had no intention of digging into his past or arguing with her. No reason to ruin the day. "At least Eddie will have that." His fingers spasmed as he thought of something. Would Eddie want—even need—brothers and sisters? But they would have Kent and Sally to fill that need.

They rattled past the place where Blaze and Emma had picked them up after their night out in the cold. In the hopes of distracting her from realizing it, he pointed ahead. "I see some flowers."

She leaned forward. "I've seen those red ones before, but I don't know what they are called."

"Indian paintbrush."

Slowly she came round to face him. "How do you know that?"

Pleased that he had drawn her attention away from realizing they passed the spot where they'd been rescued, he grinned. "A native couple visited me one winter and taught me all sorts of things."

She continued to study him. "How long did they visit?"

"Oh, maybe a month or two more or less."

"A month or two?" She narrowed her eyes. "You see, this is why we need to get to know each other better. So you weren't always alone up on your mountain?"

"Mostly I was."

"Tell me about this couple."

"What do you want to know?"

"Everything."

"Well, I don't know everything about them."

"Finn!"

He grinned. It felt good to tease someone and have them enjoy it. "Very well. Their names were Cloud and Awena. Awena means 'the sun rises.'"

"That's beautiful."

"They stayed with me about three months. Awena had been sick and was too weak to travel. They became good friends. Cloud taught me how to trap and hunt and make snowshoes. Awena taught me how to make fur-lined mittens and moccasins."

"Sounds nice. And they told you about flowers?"

"It came up when they taught me what plants were safe to eat. The Indian paintbrush is one that is."

As they passed the area, she studied the flowers scattered among the grasses next to the grove of trees.

"I suppose they're named paintbrush because they look a little like one."

"I guess they do, but that's not how they got their name."

"Really?"

"Yup." He settled back as if the conversation was over although he hoped it wasn't.

She watched him, waiting, and after a moment said with some impatience, "You're going to tell me, aren't you?"

He held back his grin at her impatience. "Tell you what?"

She jabbed him in the ribs.

He caught her fingers and held tight so she couldn't do it again and immediately warmth from where his flesh connected with hers rushed through him. Her gaze fused with his. His heart hammered in his ears.

She swallowed audibly and shifted so her hand withdrew. "About the paintbrush." Either her voice was thicker than usual, or his hearing was faulty.

The paintbrush? What was she talking about? And then he remembered. "Ah yes. How the flower got its name. According to Awena, a native maiden once fell in love with a wounded prisoner she was tending only to learn her tribe wanted him to get better so they could torture him." Seems he and Jenny weren't the only pair who had to face their community. Except they were doing it for appearance's sake, not for love.

He continued. "She helped him escape even though

she knew she would be harshly punished. She stayed with her lover for some time but missed her home so went back, where she overheard two braves discussing what would happen if they found her. It is said she took a piece of bark, gashed her leg, and used the blood to draw a picture of her former home on the piece of wood. Then she fled back to her lover's camp. She dropped the wood on her journey and where it landed, a little plant grew with a brush-like end, dyed red with her blood."

Silence followed his telling of the story. He watched her out of the corner of his eye. She stared straight ahead, her hands clasped tightly together.

"I'm sorry," he said. "It's really not a very good story."

"It's sad."

"Jenny, you don't have to be like that maiden."

She faced him. "What do you mean?"

"You don't have to choose between marrying me and following your heart."

Her expression softened. Little lines fanned out from her eyes as if she was pleased. Or amused. "Finn, when we marry…"

At least she'd said when, not if, and he drew in a satisfying breath.

"It will be because we have *both* agreed that it is what we want."

"Good to know."

"Did you think I had changed my mind since yesterday?" Her gaze sought something, though he couldn't think what. All he could do was answer the question as honestly as possible.

"You're free to change your mind. And I wouldn't blame you. After all…" He wouldn't say because he had nothing to offer, because if she was to ever to contradict that, he wanted it to come from her unbidden, unprompted, and not out of pity. "After all, we hardly know each other."

She patted his arm. "I'm learning lots about you today." She sat back, seemingly content with her decision.

Determined to change the subject to something less personal, he pointed out the hawk flying overhead, slowed the wagon to let her admire a deer bouncing over the grass.

"Do you know why these are called the Porcupine Hills?" he asked.

"Another story. Oh, good. I assume this one is about animals?"

"Wrong. It's not a story at all, though of course you would think so. Nope. Look at the hill." He pointed to a perfect example to their right. "See how it looks like a crouching porcupine, and the trees on the crest resemble quills?"

She squinted. "Yes, I see it." She brought her gaze to him. "Finn, thank you for sharing your knowledge with me."

"You're welcome. I could say the same for you. Thank you for sharing your knowledge."

"What? Did I teach you to bake bread or make a

butterscotch pudding? Oh, are you referring to digging up buffalo beans?"

"I meant the Bible verse you told me yesterday. About the Lord rejoicing over me. Except…" How did he say it without sounding critical? "I couldn't find it."

"I looked and I couldn't either. Maybe I was making it up. I'm sorry."

"No need to be sorry. You know what? The Hoopers know a lot about the Bible. I'll ask them."

The rest of the trip passed far too quickly in Finn's opinion. Being with her, the two of them alone, felt different than anything he'd ever experienced before.

* * *

JENNY TRIED NOT to show her nervousness as they rattled across a narrow bridge.

"Hooper's Coulee," Finn said. "We're almost there."

They crossed a grassy area, entered some trees. As soon as they left the trees, the house was in plain view.

"Are you sure they won't mind me showing up? The last time I did so—" She bit back the rest of what she started to say. The last time had taken her to the Stanley house and Mr. Stanley's unwelcome attentions. She hoped she managed to hide her shudder. Realized she pressed her palms to her chest, even knowing how futile such a gesture was, and lowered her hands to her lap.

"The Hoopers are good people. I don't think they'll

judge you for anything. Especially things you have no control over."

They approached the house. A bunch of people sat on the open porch and rose to watch the wagon approach. As soon as they recognized Finn and Jenny the men jumped to the ground and trotted over to greet them.

Finn helped Jenny down and she was immediately surrounded by the women. Two little girls and a boy watched the proceedings. She knew their names. Rosie, the almost one year old, stood by a chair, holding it to keep her balance. Meg, the oldest one, rested her hand on the big furry dog who rose to watch them. The other dog, a big yellow animal, stayed with the women, pressing close to Emma. Ian, slightly older than Rosie, sat on the porch floor, banging a spoon on the floor and laughing at the noise.

"Are you all right today?" Emma asked.

"We heard about your accident." Connie squeezed her hand.

"Glad you weren't hurt more seriously," Theresa said.

"Ladies." Blaze was gently chiding. "Let them come to the porch."

Jenny glanced at Finn, saw the tiny smile as he met her gaze. He seemed to say she was in good hands, and she relaxed.

They were served coffee and cookies. After the usual pleasantries there was a lull in the conversation.

Jenny glanced around the circle. Perhaps they were curious about what had happened after Blaze and Emma left town yesterday. She looked at Finn. Was he going to tell them? After all, he knew them better than she did.

He gave a slight nod. "I suppose you're all wondering what was decided about our situation?"

Several of them looked away as if not wanting to admit their curiosity. "Blaze, you and Emma were there to hear what was said when we first got there."

"We heard," Blaze said. "I told the others. We've been concerned for you."

"Jenny and I have agreed to marry."

The words echoed in the silence.

Should she try and explain? But how? What could she say? And would they understand or judge them?

"I hope it's not because a bunch of nosy bodies think you should." Levi swept his arms upward as if driving off the comments of such people.

Jenny sent Finn a pleading look. *Say something. Explain our decision.*

Something about the way his eyes dipped at the corners caused her to think he understood. He held her gaze as he began to speak. "We discussed it and agree that we will marry. Yes, in part to protect Jenny's reputation. But we have our own reasons as well."

Levi leaned forward. "Do you love each other? It's the only reason to get married."

Jenny's cheeks grew warm at the way Finn kept

looking at her. Was he trying to convince the others they were in love?

"We're learning to appreciate each other." He shifted his attention to the others. "But there's also a little boy who needs a home, and we've agreed we can give him one." He waited for the ensuing uproar to subside then explained about Eddie.

"He'll be a fortunate boy," Theresa said. "To have two people prepared to sacrifice their own future for his well-being."

"Every child deserves to be taken care of by good people." Finn nodded toward the three children.

Jenny knew they'd all been adopted into the Hooper family.

Cash scooped up Rosie and she nuzzled her face into his neck. "I couldn't agree more."

That brought an end to the interrogation.

Blaze stood. "We welcome Jenny and Finn to our Sunday service. Jenny, Finn has been here before so perhaps he's told you about our practice."

"He did. I'm looking forward to being a part of it."

"Good. Then let's begin." The chairs were shuffled around, each man sitting beside his wife. That left Finn to sit beside Jenny. Not that she minded. It made her feel like she belonged with the others.

Blaze stood before them. "We'll open with prayer." He bowed his head and prayed. "Amen. What song shall we sing?"

Levi called out, "'O God, Our Help in Ages Past.'"

The Hoopers sang.

Jenny had never heard more beautiful singing. The men all had lovely voices and the women's voices added sweet overtones. She was only slightly familiar with the words and was happy to listen. Finn remained silent. She'd have to ask him why he didn't join in. Was it because he didn't know the words or because he was afraid to be heard by the others?

The song ended. Little Meg fussed and Jake picked her up and settled her on his knee.

Blaze watched the pair. "We'll cut this short before the little ones grow too weary. Levi, did you have something to share with us today?" Blaze sat down and Levi took his place.

"You all remember how Ma taught us to memorize scripture?"

The men murmured agreement.

"This week, two of the verses I'd learned seemed to come together in my mind. 'I have loved thee with an everlasting love: therefore with lovingkindness have I drawn thee.'"

The four men murmured together, "Jeremiah chapter thirty-one, verse three."

Levi continued. "And the verse that says 'Who shall separate us from the love of Christ? shall tribulation, or distress, or persecution, or famine, or nakedness, or peril, or sword?'"

Again the four of them murmured, "Romans chapter eight, verse thirty-five."

"We know the answer. Nothing in heaven or on

earth can separate us from God's love. We need to remember that."

Levi's expression serious, he looked at each of them.

The words he had spoken seared into Jenny's heart.

The meeting was over so abruptly, Jenny felt off balance. Or was the bump on her head still bothering her? She touched her forehead. The bruise was tender.

Finn leaned close, his words for her alone. "Is your head bothering you? We can leave if you want."

"No. I'm fine." She held her eyes wide and pushed the feeling away. Later, she'd think about what Levi had said.

Finn turned to the others. "I'm hoping you can help me find a verse. Something about the Lord rejoicing over you."

"I know the one you mean." Blaze opened his Bible. "It's in Zephaniah."

"Zeph a who?" Finn said, earning him a laugh from the others.

"Here it is." Blaze read aloud, "'He will rejoice over thee with joy.' And the last phrase, 'He will joy over thee with singing.' Those beautiful verses are right here in Zephaniah chapter three, verse seventeen." He showed the page to Finn.

Finn murmured the reference over several times. "I want to be able to look it up when I get back."

"That verse would make a good song," Theresa said.

The ladies murmured agreement then said they

must look after the food and headed for the kitchen. Jenny hurried after them. She saw a table laden with dishes filled with food.

"I didn't bring anything to contribute to the meal." She should have thought.

"Pshaw. Look at all this. We always worry there won't be enough, and we end up able to feed an army."

"Please stay," Theresa said.

Zola and Connie added their welcome.

Jenny nodded. "Thank you." Then as an afterthought, "Perhaps I should ask Finn if he plans to stay."

"By all means." Theresa nodded toward the porch where the men talked. "But I've never known a man to refuse a meal. Have any of you?" She looked to her sisters-in-law.

They grinned. "Not once," Emma said.

Zola chuckled. "I'd think Levi was ill if he refused a meal."

The others laughed. "We'd all know he was ill if he refused a second helping."

Jenny relaxed. "I expect you're right. Now what can I do to help?"

"Would you slice a loaf of bread?"

A few minutes later the men joined them. Blaze offered a prayer of thanksgiving then they dished up and went outside to eat.

"It's so pleasant here," Jenny said.

"Maybe you two will choose to live on a ranch." Blaze's words opened up a wide ache inside Jenny.

She'd told herself she didn't ever plan to marry. Then, because of circumstances they had no control over, she had agreed to marry Finn. But sitting here looking out at the rolling hills, watching the children play, seeing the dogs keeping guard, a long-buried dream resurfaced.

How often, late at night, just before she fell asleep, had she imagined herself standing in the doorway of a house, watching a man trot toward her? A man who loved her and who had fathered the children gathered at her side?

It was a dream she must put to rest forever if she married Finn.

She breathed slowly, pushing the dream back behind closed doors.

The meal ended. The men went to look at the horses. The women brought out a quilt they were working on in memory of the men's mother.

Jenny did her best to stay involved in the conversation but her mind kept drifting to forbidden dreams.

15

*F*inn was glad enough to look at the Hooper horses. He'd always enjoyed riding such animals and working with them. If he allowed himself regrets, not having a horse or two would be one.

They returned to the house. He saw the other women without really seeing them, but Jenny was clear as early morning sunshine. She wore a troubled look. Had someone done or said something to upset her? He took a step toward her then stopped. He didn't have the right. Not yet. But as soon as it seemed polite, he said, "Perhaps we should be on our way back." Then with a weak attempt at humor, he added, "Wouldn't want to end up being out after dark."

At least the men found his comment amusing.

Jenny got to her feet and walked across the porch. At the steps, he held out his hand to assist her. Her fingers were cool in his. He studied her closely as she descended, and he led her to the wagon.

She met his gaze. He wasn't sure what he saw in the murky green depths of her eyes, but whatever it was made him squeeze her hand and give her what he hoped was an encouraging smile. He was rewarded when her eyes cleared, and she smiled.

He helped her to the seat, then took his place beside her. They thanked the Hoopers for their hospitality, bade them good-bye then drove away.

They rode in silence until they crossed the bridge.

"You looked upset back there. Did someone say something to you?"

"Me? No, I wasn't upset." She straightened her shoulders and smoothed her skirts.

"You're certain?" He knew what he'd seen and waited, suspecting she was only pretending.

Slowly the starch went out of her and she slumped forward. "If you must know, being there reminded me of a long-ago dream. It was sad to remember it and know it would never be."

"Jenny, why can't it ever be?" He'd help her find her dream if it was in his power.

"It just can't."

"I'd sure like to hear it."

She stiffened again.

He continued, his voice soft. "I thought the whole idea was to get to know each other better."

She stared straight ahead, giving no indication if she heard, though she must have. After a moment, she looked to her right, away from Finn. Then she picked at imaginary flecks of lint on her skirt.

He waited. She must choose how much she wanted him to know of her. Then, as if realizing what she did, she clasped her hands together. They rode on in silence apart from the rattle of the harness and the clomp, clomp of the horses' hooves.

She shifted to face him. The movement so sudden, it made Finn's fingers curl tightly.

"I'll tell you my dream if you promise to tell me something about yourself. Preferably a dream." Her gaze was insistent, demanding, pleading.

"What if I don't have any dreams?"

She lifted one shoulder. "That's my condition. If you have nothing to share, neither do I." She held his gaze in a vise. He couldn't break free.

"You drive a hard bargain."

"Take it or leave it." She faced forward again.

"I'll take it." He'd think of something to tell her.

She groaned. "I was hoping you'd say no."

"A deal is a deal."

"Very well. Being at the Hoopers' ranch reminded me of a dream I had when I was young. Much younger." Her voice halting, she told about how she imagined living on a ranch, sharing her life with a man who loved her, and the children they had together.

"I can't take that dream from you."

"Finn, it's an old dream. A childish dream. Besides, the Stanleys took that dream from me. Not you."

He touched her shoulder, felt her shiver beneath his palm. "I'll do my best to fulfill your dream."

She shrugged from under his hand. "We both know what we've agreed to. I don't expect any more than that."

He returned his hand to the reins. If he could, he would offer her everything in her dream along with the sun to shine in the daytime and the moon to light her path at night. But the only thing he could give her was the protection of her good name and a little boy. It had to be enough.

For a time, they were both content to settle into their own thoughts and watch the passing scenery.

She stretched her arms and arched her back and yawned. Then faced him. "Now it's your turn."

He knew what she meant but hoped to divert her. "Did you enjoy visiting the Hoopers?"

"Of course, they are a lovely family. But don't try and change the subject."

"Something they said kind of bothers me."

That made her forget her demands. "I can't imagine what."

"They said you were sacrificing your future. I don't want you to do that."

"Since when do you care what others think?"

"I care what the Hoopers think." There was something more, and he managed to squeeze out the words. "I care what people will think about you and me spending the night together."

"Are you changing your mind about marriage?"

"No. But I'd understand if you do."

"Well, I'm not. A deal is a deal. Now tell me a dream of yours."

"Very well." The conversation had reminded him of one. "When I was a child, living at the Moores, I would watch Ethel sitting at the table with her parents or running down the path to them as she returned from school. I wanted to have that too. That welcome. That belonging. It's too late for me now, but it's what I want for Eddie." He'd never before acknowledged, even to himself, what he wanted for the boy.

"We can give him that."

He squeezed her hand. "Agreed." But did their plans include standing side by side to welcome the boy home, to walk him to church, or even to take him on outings?

"I wonder what he's like."

"I do, too. He should be here soon, and we'll find out."

They sank into thoughtful silence for the space of a mile or two. Then she stirred. "Finn, I'm glad Blaze could show you where that Bible verse was."

"Me, too." Zephaniah three, seventeen. He'd look it up in his own Bible as soon as he could. "But I gotta ask, who would name their son Zephaniah? That's a real mouthful."

She laughed. "I've never heard of anyone with it apart from in the Bible."

"Good thing."

She studied him a moment. "What were your parents' names?"

"Ma and Pa."

That earned him a chuckle. "I doubt everyone called them that."

"I only heard other people call them Mr. and Mrs. Johnson." Something fluttered through his brain. "I might have heard someone call my pa Ralph. Or am I only thinking that because you said it was your brother's name?"

Jenny patted his arm. "Ralph is a good name. I wish you could meet my brother. You'd like him."

"But would he like me?"

Her gaze skimmed over his cheeks, his beard—at least he'd had it trimmed—his mouth and came to rest on his eyes. "I can't see any reason he wouldn't." Pink like the fairest of wild roses blossomed in her cheeks. She turned to face straight ahead.

He settled back for the rest of the drive home, satisfied with how the day had gone.

They reached town. He took her to the back of the café and helped her down. Bill watched from the grassy area with the children playing nearby.

"You'll join us for supper, won't you?"

He'd like to but...

"A deal is a deal."

Put that way, he didn't know if she referred to the fencing arrangement or their decision to get to know each other better. "Thanks. I'll be back as soon as I return the wagon."

At the livery he faced Big Sam, who blocked his way. "You been courtin' that gal?"

"You might say that." It wasn't the term either he or Jenny used but let others think what they wanted.

"Just until the Mountie gets back." It wasn't a question but an order.

Finn wouldn't let the man push him around. Not that he could stop him. Big Sam was a good hundred pounds heavier than Finn, with arms like oak trees, and Finn wasn't about to argue. "That's what we agreed on. You know that."

"Wouldn't want *you* forgettin' it." He jabbed his sausage-sized finger at Finn.

"Don't intend to." He could think of no reason why he wouldn't gladly enter into marriage with Jenny. She was good company. He felt more at ease talking to her than anyone else he'd ever known. Besides, they'd agreed to give Eddie a home.

It wasn't until he was on his way back to the café that he remembered he intended to go back to his mountain cabin. Not that he'd changed his mind. After all, they didn't have a home in town.

But he had offered to build her a house.

Too bad he couldn't give her a place in the country, on a ranch, like she'd once dreamt of.

JENNY HUSTLED about the kitchen Monday morning. There were dozens of things to do. Biscuits to make.

Cookies, too. Hilda planned soup for the noon meal to go with the biscuits. Jenny had agreed to chop vegetables for that. At least that task allowed her to be near the window where she could watch Finn work on the fence. He was methodical in his labor. That was something she admired. No rush. No going back and forth to get something he'd forgotten or redoing a mistake.

Laura stood next to her. "For your sake, I hope he is a good man and doesn't pretend one thing and do another."

Jenny could say she believed Finn to be a man of his word. He'd promised to marry her. Said that together they would give Eddie a home. He'd gone so far as to offer to build her a house in town. But he'd not promised anything more. Not a home together. Not a real family. Not that it mattered to her. She'd given up her dreams when she left behind the gossip and unkind remarks of the Stanley men. It was only going to the Hooper ranch that brought them to the fore again. "I have to take him at his word."

Laura leaned closer to the window. "It would be nice to feel you can trust him though. Especially seeing as you plan to marry him. And in such a hurry."

"Do we have a choice?"

"No, I suppose you don't. Still..." Laura left to return to her own chores.

Jenny continued to work. She dumped the chopped vegetables into the pot and filled a cup with coffee. "I'm going to take this to Finn."

Hilda gave her a considering look but didn't say anything.

Jenny couldn't explain the sudden need to talk to Finn. Except he always seemed so rational. Made her feel they were doing the right thing.

He looked up with a smile of welcome as she approached. He took the coffee she offered. "Thanks." After a few swallows he turned toward the fence. "How does it look?"

"Good. I can see how it'll block the wind. My garden thanks you and so do I."

There was something different about the way he smiled at her today. Or was it only in her mind?

"Are we doing the right thing?" she blurted out.

He blinked. His smile flattened and she regretted having said the words aloud. "Jenny, no one can force you to marry me. And I wouldn't want that. It is the right thing to do for your reputation and for Eddie. But if it isn't what you want, then don't be afraid to say so." He waited, but she couldn't say what she wanted.

"What's really troubling you?" he asked when she didn't reply.

"I don't know. I guess it's because—Finn, what if I can't be a wife to you or a mother to Eddie? What if—" She fluttered her hands, not even knowing why she was so confused and uncertain.

Finn set his now-empty cup on the pile of wood and took her hand to lead her to the shelter of the shed. "Sit, and we'll talk."

She sank to the ground, grateful he sat beside her, his shoulder against hers. Already her inner turmoil had begun to settle just being with him.

"Jenny, are you still listening to the lies the Stanley men said? Worse, believing them?"

"I suppose I am."

"Does having them say something make it true?" His calm words soothed her.

"I don't suppose it does."

"Think about all you have done and can do. You cook and bake and help with meals. You help with the children. You plant a garden that is thriving under your care." He turned to face her and took her hands. "Jenny, you're like your garden."

"Huh? How? It's dirt and plants."

"Take a good look. What are those rows?"

"Carrots and beans."

"Nothing very pretty about them. They're practical. Useful. Necessary to provide food."

She nodded, wondering where he was going with this.

"Now look at the flowers against the house." There was a smattering of flowers blooming.

"They're pretty."

"They give us all pleasure, don't they?"

Again, she nodded.

"You're like your garden. Able to do practical things, take care of others, help where needed, but you're also beautiful like the flowers. One isn't any better than the other. Both are appreciated."

She stared into his face. Felt herself sinking into the golden-brown depths of his eyes. Warmed by his approval. She tried to speak but all that came out was a squeak. She cleared her throat. "Finn, that was so nice. Thank you."

He sat back against the shed. "You're welcome, but it's the truth as I see it."

"Thank you," she whispered. "Finn, I do want to marry you. You make me feel safe and—" She stopped before she uttered the word, *valued*.

"Good to know. In the interest of getting to know each other better, why don't we go for a walk after supper when you're free?"

"I'd like that."

"I suppose we should get back to our work." He rose and pulled her to her feet.

She stood before him, drinking in the strength and kindness his gaze offered.

He touched her cheek. "I'll see you later."

Her face warm, she hurried toward the house. What had just happened?

16

---

       *F*inn watched Jenny return to the house then went back to building the fence. It would soon be finished. No doubt the Mountie would return within a few days. And then what? He would have to stay until Eddie arrived. Or would he? Yes, he would. He couldn't imagine leaving Jenny to sort out everything on her own. Besides, he wanted to see the boy. Would he be lost and afraid, as Finn was when he was orphaned? It was something Finn might be able to help the boy with. For sure, he wouldn't use the boy as a slave. Nor would he allow anyone else to do so. Not that he feared Jenny would do that. She'd expressed shock at how Finn had been treated, and he'd observed her with Kent and Sally. Always kind. Teaching them without driving them.

He would stay until the boy was settled.

That raised another question. Did he continue to

camp by the river, or build a house? What would Jenny want? He'd ask her.

He'd taught himself to dwell only with the problems at hand—like where to get his next meal, did he have enough firewood, had a bear been prowling near his cabin?—and now his thoughts were scattered near and far. Though perhaps not so far. Just to Jenny and their plans.

He ate both dinner and supper outdoors, pleading the need to keep at the fence but really, he didn't want to go inside and be forced to be part of a family gathering. More and more he was finding himself longing for what he saw and could never have.

In the back of his mind, a question reared its head. Why couldn't he have it?

Was it because he was afraid?

He pushed aside the questions and slipped away to wash up at the creek then he returned to meet Jenny. They turned their steps toward the creek where they could spend some time without fear of curious spectators.

They walked along the bank.

"Jenny, I think I should stay in town until Eddie arrives."

"I think you should, too. For one thing, he needs to know you care about him."

It was a little hard to care about someone he'd never met and knew nothing about except who his mother was. But he understood what she meant. "I'll stay until he's settled and comfortable with us. You."

"Shouldn't he be here soon?"

"I would think so. Too bad Ethel didn't think to provide a little information about his arrival."

"Seems odd."

"Ethel is used to people willing to wait on her."

"Hmm."

Finn chuckled. "I know you mean that to sound indifferent, but I think I hear a touch of disapproval in your tone."

She wrinkled her nose. "You likely do."

Ahead of them, a lad of about twelve stood on the bank fishing. They stopped a distance away to watch without disturbing the boy.

"I used to go with Ralph when he fished. I would sit on the bank and play with the rocks and watch bugs and chase butterflies."

Finn ground to a halt and stared at the young fisherman.

Jenny touched his arm. "Finn, what's wrong?"

He swallowed hard. "I remember."

"Yes?"

"My pa took me fishing. I remember that. I caught a little trout that Ma fried for our supper." He turned to stare at Jenny. "I remember."

She squeezed his arm. "I'm glad for you. It's good for you to recall your life before the Moores. How does it feel?"

"I don't know. It's like a door to a sun-filled room has opened. I can't see for the brightness."

"Finn." She rubbed his arm. "It's good to remember you were a loved child."

He nodded. He could believe that.

She touched his chin to bring his gaze to her. "You are worthy of love now, too."

He stared into her eyes. What did she mean? Love wasn't part of their arrangement. Nor did he think he was capable of it. Too long deprived of it to truly know what it was. Having no reply for her, he resumed walking along the creek, with her at his side.

He couldn't say what they talked about the rest of the evening as his thoughts loosened and tightened like someone was turning a screw in his head. The light, the memories. The lessons to keep his head down, mind his own business, expect nothing. Back and forth. Back and forth. Open and closed. Open and closed.

It was a most unsettling feeling, and he took Jenny home and hurried back to the camp where Bill munched grass contentedly.

He envied his mule's calm acceptance of his life. Taking affection and attention where he could find it then grazing grass with no thought in his head. Just content to be a mule.

* * *

JENNY LAY on her bed careful not to toss and turn and alert the others to her state of mind. Why had Finn been so upset at remembering life with his family?

Why was he so willing to believe he wasn't worthy of love?

But he was. He deserved to be loved so completely that his time with the Moores would become nothing more than a distant memory without shape or substance.

She could give him that. Despite his determination to be distant, he was a truly nice man. He would be easy to love. In fact, she might be falling in love with him even now. Not that she'd admit it to anyone, especially Finn. It would scare him back to his mountain.

She smiled into the darkness. Actions spoke louder than words.

THE NEXT MORNING, she waited for him to show up, and practically dragged him inside for breakfast.

"I ate at my camp," he protested.

"Did you light a fire?"

He admitted he hadn't.

"Then you haven't had a decent breakfast. Sit here." She pointed to the table in the kitchen. "I'll make you something."

Hilda studied her a moment then shrugged. Laura wore a troubled look but said nothing. Delcie—*oh please, Delcie, don't say anything cruel*—gave them both a sour look then took the children to her bedroom on the excuse they needed to do lessons.

Kent protested until Delcie whispered something in his ear.

Meanwhile, Jenny worked on breakfast. Coffee was ready and she took him a cupful. In a few minutes, she had a stack of pancakes and put the plate before him along with fresh butter and syrup. Before he finished that, she had crisp bacon and four fried eggs, which she served with fresh bread.

He stared at the food. "What are you doing?"

"Showing you that I can cook?"

Laura laughed. "The way to a man's heart is through his stomach."

Jenny sent her a warning look. "Is that right? I guess I wouldn't know."

She sat across from Finn. "What are your plans for the day?"

"Work on the fence." He eyed her. "Did you have something else in mind?"

Her cheeks warmed as she thought of the things she'd like to do. Go on a picnic. Long walk along the creek. Pick flowers. "Nope. Just making conversation."

He cleaned his plate and pushed it aside. "That was the best breakfast I've ever had. Thank you."

"You're welcome. Talk to you later," she said before he went out the door.

"Jennifer Lyster, that was blatant flirting," Laura scolded.

"How can you say that? We feed people—mostly men—every day. Is that flirting?" She hoped any color in her cheeks could be put down to washing the dishes in hot water.

"It's different, and you know it."

So what if she did?

"Leave the gal alone." Hilda waved her wooden spoon around. "She's planning to marry the man. I should hope there'd be a few sparks flying."

Jenny ducked her head to hide the heat racing to her cheeks.

Laura sighed. "I hope she won't regret it."

Delcie came from the room and shooed the children outside. "We will make sure he doesn't hurt her."

Jenny knew that none of them could prevent the kind of hurt that words and disappointments could inflict.

Finn worked steadily on the fence and refused to come in when Kent called him for dinner.

"He says he wants to keep working," Kent said.

"But the man has to eat."

Hilda looked ready to go out and drag him in.

"Let it be," Jenny said. "I'll take something out to him." She dished up two plates and went to his side. "I brought food," she said.

"You didn't need to."

"No one made me do it."

That brought his head up and he met her gaze. *Oh, Finn. Why can't you believe you're good for more than your work?* But she'd decided to use actions rather than words.

He wiped his hands on his trousers and joined her beside the shed where they both sat in the shade.

For a few minutes, they ate in silence.

Jenny finished first. "You're a good carpenter."

"It's a fence. Anyone can build one."

"But didn't you say you built your cabin?" She recalled something he had said. "Who taught you to build things?" He'd mentioned that his pa had been helping him build a little barn.

His chewing stopped. He swallowed audibly. "My Pa." His words were very soft.

"Don't you think he'd be pleased to know his lessons meant something to you?" So much for not using her words.

"I don't know." She could barely hear him.

She decided it was wisest to let it go. For now.

A few minutes later, he handed her his empty plate, thanked her, and returned to the fence.

That evening, he didn't ask her to walk with him. Rather, he worked on the fence until almost dark. As if to prove work was all that mattered.

THE NEXT DAY, she decided she would prove otherwise to him. She prepared a picnic lunch then went out to ask him to help her dig out some plants. He looked about ready to refuse.

"I don't think I can do it myself."

He looked at the fence. "Very well." He set aside the tools and went to get the bucket and shovel. She slipped into the house and got the picnic basket, ignoring the looks her friends gave her.

"What's this?" he asked when she rejoined him.

"Our lunch so we don't need to hurry back."

"I see."

She doubted he did.

"Do you want to take a wagon? I could get one from the livery."

"I want to explore along the creek. It's not suitable for a wagon."

"Very well."

They walked down the street to the creek. They had been this way a couple of nights ago. This time she meant to go farther.

"What are you looking for?" he asked after a bit when their conversation had been limited to comments about the scenery and birds.

"I want a little pine tree to plant beside the shed."

"I don't see any here."

"Then we'll have to go farther."

They walked on, for the most part in silence, until she felt like her ears would burst from the sound of it.

"There's one." He pointed.

"It'll do." She let him dig until the little tree was loose with a good-sized lump of dirt clinging to its roots. He put it in the pail.

"We might as well eat before we head back." She went to a grassy area. He followed and they sat side by side. She opened the basket then looked to him. "Would you ask the blessing?"

His jaw muscles bunched. For a moment she thought he would refuse, but then he bowed his head. "Thanks for food. Amen."

She lifted her head.

He did not.

She waited. *Please, God, help him let go of the ugly parts of his past and embrace the good parts.* Like when he had a loving family. She had promised herself to be silent and let her deeds speak to him, but she couldn't. "'He will rejoice over thee with joy. He will joy over thee with singing.'"

Slowly his head came up. His eyes filled with darkness. "It's not always easy to believe those words."

"Finn, you've made me see that I shouldn't put so much stock in what the Stanleys said." She didn't say anything more, wanting him to see the same truth she had about what others said.

He blinked twice. Opened and closed his mouth before he spoke. "And I'm being foolish to believe Mr. Moore's words above God's. To believe what he taught you above what Pa taught me."

"And you aren't a foolish man." She was rewarded by seeing his eyes brighten and the tiny lines fanning out from his eyes deepen.

"I think I have been. Jenny, thank you for making me see that I was making it difficult to believe when it's so very simple."

"Are you saying you're going to forget what Mr. Moore taught you?"

The lines around his eyes deepened even more. "Just the bad things. He did teach me the value of doing my best. And not causing trouble."

She chuckled. "That's something worth keeping." She handed him a sandwich, so grateful that Finn had chosen this path. She'd learned to like the more care-free Finn a great deal.

"You've said very little about your parents," he said. "Tell me about them."

Guessing he longed to hear about normal family life, she told him of summer evenings spent on the veranda playing word games, of learning house-keeping skills under her mother's kind instruction, of rowdy evenings playing chase with Ralph, and winter evenings around the warm fireplace with her father reading aloud to them.

"It sounds nice," he said when she finished.

"It was. I'm sorry you didn't have the same kind of childhood."

"Me, too. Did you hear how the Hoopers learned to memorize Bible verses from their mother?"

"You mentioned it before."

"After I heard that, I thought if I ever had a family, it's something I'd like to do. In fact, I've memorized a few verses since Blaze gave me a Bible."

"Good for you. Finn, you know you'll be getting a family soon. You'll soon have a wife and when Eddie comes, a son. We could teach Eddie to memorize verses. We could do it together."

At the look on his face—of both hope and despair —she knew family was still a dream he thought was out of reach.

She leaned closer and cupped her hand to his cheek. "You are Finn Johnson. Not Finn Moore."

He blinked. Caught her hand and pressed it tight to

his face. "How can you see me better than I see myself?"

She dared not say because she saw through eyes of love. "I just do."

He pulled her hand to his knee and continued to hold it. "Thank you for making me see things differently."

He patted the ground beside him, and she shifted over there. They sat side by side, leaning against a tree, and ate their lunch. Neither of them seemed in a hurry to end the day, and they stayed there most of the afternoon, talking about the hills and the flowers, talking about the Hoopers and their little ones, talking about people who had been in town on Saturday.

"Do you want your own house?" he asked.

The question caught her off guard. Yes, she wanted her own house. On a ranch. With Finn eager to come home to her. But he hadn't suggested that.

"If we had a house, it would be easier for you to visit"—stay—"when you come down from the mountain."

"I like that. As soon as I finish the fence, I'll draw up plans for a house. Is there anything in particular you'd like?"

"A house on a ranch?" she teased, hoping he took it that way.

Instead, he turned to study her. "Are you prepared to give up your dream?"

She held his gaze. If only she could tell him the dream meant nothing unless he was in it. "I was joshing. The only thing I care about is whether the house is solid and warm and that it has a big kitchen."

"I can do that." He looked into her eyes. "I'll always do my best to please you."

She lost herself in his gaze. Could she ask for anything more, anything better from him?

Only love. But this would have to be enough.

17

$\mathcal{F}$inn wished he could give Jenny more, especially after the gift she'd given him. Setting him free from the painful years he'd spent at the Moores, from the things Ethel had said. Jenny wanted a house with a big kitchen. He'd build her the best one possible, with a bay window in the living room. With bedrooms—how many? He wasn't going to think about that right now, knowing they'd agreed to a marriage in name only.

It was long past time to return to town, but he hated to stir. Sitting beside Jenny was like a tonic to his soul.

But they couldn't stay there forever. "We should get your little tree planted," he said.

"I suppose so, but I'm enjoying this too much to want to leave."

He grinned both inside and out to know she shared

his reluctance. "Your friends might send out a search party if we don't show up soon."

"More likely Big Sam will come."

They both laughed at the thought of the smithy steaming up the hill prepared to defend Jenny's honor.

"It's nice to know people care about you," he said.

"I hope you're counting yourself among those." Her eyes were hungry, and he understood her need for reassurance.

"Of course I do. I appreciate a beautiful garden." He knew by the way she smiled that she was thinking of his earlier comments. He got to his feet and held out a hand to assist her.

They stood face to face. She studied him as deeply as he studied her.

She *was* like a beautiful garden.

What was he like?

As if reading his mind, she said, "Finn, you're a mighty oak, staying strong and upright despite the storms life throws at you."

A mighty oak. He liked that.

Contentment encircling him, he escorted her back to town. She indicated where she wanted the tree. He dug a hole and planted it while she fetched water for it. They completed the job and stood back to admire the four-foot addition to the garden.

"It looks good," he said.

"When I look at it, I will remember this day."

"Me, too." His voice held a husky note. He would think of how she'd made him see that he didn't have to continue to let Mr. Moore's harshness control him.

The sound of passing horses drew his attention to the street. He recognized the rider, and his fingers knotted around the handle of the shovel.

Jenny had also turned toward the street. She stared after the rider then turned to Finn, her eyes wide and dark. "The Mountie is back."

"'Pears that way." Was she relieved or disappointed?

"That means we can get married."

"There's still time to change your mind."

Her eyes narrowed as she studied him. "I've made my decision. I'm not changing it. Are you wanting to?"

"No. I've given my word and I mean to keep it."

Her shoulders rose ever so slightly and fell again. "It would be nice to know that wasn't your only reason for doing this. That you gave your word."

He pressed his hand to her shoulder. "Jenny, I'm not minding in the least that I gave my word. I'm quite looking forward to a life shared with you." He waited for her response, hoping she wouldn't be offended by his frankness.

A smile began in the depths of her eyes and fanned out to her face. "Thank you." Her voice rounded with what he hoped was pleasure at his confession. "Now what?" She tipped her head toward the street where the Mountie was now out of sight.

"I don't know." How did one go about arranging a marriage?

At that moment, Mrs. Meyer called them in.

They looked at each other. Her eyes were steady. He hoped his were, too, for he was completely confident of what he planned to do. Marry Jenny. Build her a house that would be a home for both her and Eddie. And maybe later...

He closed the door to wanting more. Besides, that was enough.

Together they went into the kitchen where three women confronted them with stern looks on each face.

He and Jenny drew to a halt just inside the door. He kicked it closed. At least the children were out entertaining Bill and not privy to this.

"I see the Mountie has returned." Miss Morton's voice informed them she expected them to get right over there and tend to this marriage business.

"You can now get married." At least Mrs. Meyer was kindly enough.

"Just be sure..."

Miss Morton's warning look cut off what Miss Fisher meant to say.

Jenny crossed her arms and faced her friends. "I get the feeling you're trying to rush me. Well, I won't be rushed. Finn and I will decide when. I most certainly am not marching over there before the corporal even has time to wash his face and enjoy a cup of coffee."

"Have you decided ven?"

"You didn't give us a chance to decide. We've barely had time to realize he's back."

Finn admired her for the way she stood up to the

others. He was about to suggest he and Jenny go back out and talk when the door to the dining area banged open and Big Sam bellowed, "Where is that Finn Johnson? He's got no more excuse for putting off that wedding."

Finn chuckled at the way Jenny tossed her hands in the air.

She marched forward, pushed past her friends, and strode into the dining room. "Howdy, Sam. What can we do for you?"

Finn followed with the ladies pressing behind him.

Big Sam jabbed his meaty finger toward Finn. "No more excuses."

Finn didn't get a chance to even open his mouth before Jenny went toe-to-toe with the big man. He shivered at the contrast in size.

Though one looked as stubborn and angry as the other.

Jenny jabbed her slender finger toward Big Sam.

Finn gulped. The man could crush every bone in her hand if he took the notion.

"Sam." Her voice was strong and clear. "You've pushed us quite enough. Finn and I are getting married. Not because—" Jab jab. Not quite touching him but making him draw back. "—you say so. But because we agreed to. If you're anxious to attend the wedding, you're welcome to. If it meets with the Mountie's approval, the wedding will take place right here." She jabbed her finger toward the floor. "At three o'clock tomorrow." With a huff, she turned from the startled man, grabbed Finn's arm, and half dragged him across the floor and out the door, not slowing until they were at the far side of the shed. Her air whooshed out.

"I can't believe I did that." She chuckled. "Sure surprised Sam, didn't I? Surprised myself, too."

"Surprised me, too." Finn pressed his hands to her shoulders. "Sure glad I didn't have to come between the two of you."

She lifted her gaze to his, unblinking. Full of humor, determination, and something that made his heart pick up speed. He couldn't say what he thought he saw. Only that it made him dream of possibilities.

"I'm sorry," she said. "I didn't ask you before I made my grand announcement. Is tomorrow afternoon good for you?"

"It's fine." He had no idea what he needed to do in preparation for a wedding. Only one thing came to mind. "I'll go talk to the Mountie."

She shifted her attention to the street, and he managed to step back and cross to the Mountie's office.

A few minutes later, he emerged from the NWMP building just as a stagecoach rumbled to a stop next door. He waited for the dust to settle then with a thought that Eddie might be on the coach, he changed direction. Just in time to see a young boy jump down. Smallish and thin with a mop of curly blond hair pushing out in every direction from his cap. The boy turned around and waited as the driver helped a woman down.

Finn ground to a halt and stared. It couldn't be. But it was.

Ethel Moore, though now Mrs. Hankins. Widow Hankins. Looking as well dressed as ever. She thanked the driver, shook her skirts to dislodge the dust, and looked around.

She saw Finn. Blinked. Squinted. "Finn?" She lifted her skirts, closed the few yards between them and hugged him. "Finn, I'm so glad to see you. I should never have sent you away. It was the biggest mistake of my life. Thank goodness I've found you."

The stagecoach drove away, leaving the two of them hugging openly.

Across the street, Jenny watched. Even at this distance he could see the shock in her face. And then she hurried into her house.

Ethel eased away and sniffed into a lace-trimmed hankie. "I'm sorry for being so emotional." She smiled at the boy. "This is my son, Eddie. Eddie, come say hello to Mr. Johnson. He's the man I told you about."

Finn would like to know what she'd said to her son. How did anyone explain to a child that he was about to be left an orphan?

Eddie's gaze went from his mother to Finn and back to his mother. His eyes were blue, full of caution.

Finn's heart went out to the boy. "I mean you no harm."

Eddie nodded, but his expression plainly said he wasn't prepared to believe Finn just yet.

"Is there someplace we can talk?" Ethel asked.

Finn heard the weariness in her voice, saw how her hand shook. The only place taking in visitors was the stopping house they stood in front of, and it was as crude as ever. No place for a lady. Where would she stay? And for how long? But for now, she needed to sit and no doubt, eat.

"We'll go to the café across the street." It would give Jenny a chance to meet Eddie. A chance to change her mind before it was too late.

Ethel clung to his arm with Eddie hanging on her other hand as they went into the café.

It was Miss Fisher who brought them food and tea.

He looked through the open door to the kitchen but didn't see Jenny. He listened to Ethel's complaints about the trip with half an ear. Where was Jenny? Had she already changed her mind?

LAURA SAT on the edge of Jenny's bed where Jenny lay, her back to the room. "Shouldn't you at least say hello to his friend?" Laura said.

"I can't. This is the woman he's loved since his youth."

Ethel had said she was dying. She looked perfectly healthy to Jenny. Blonde and blue-eyed, her complexion perhaps a bit too pale, but with an air of self-confidence that almost frightened Jenny. Had her letter simply been a ruse to get Finn to stay in Willow Creek until she arrived?

"I can't stand in his way."

"You think he wants to marry her?" Laura didn't sound surprised so much as resigned. Who could blame her? She'd been duped by a man claiming to love two women.

"Why wouldn't he? It was her rejection that turned him into a mountain man."

Laura gave a mirthless chuckle. "I guess women aren't the only ones to be wounded in matters of the heart."

"How comforting to know."

Laura patted Jenny's arm. "You can't hide in here forever."

"Hmm. Maybe I'll become a mountain woman."

With a startled laugh, Laura left the room.

Jenny shifted to her back and stared at the ceiling. She would not let Finn feel obligated to marry her when Ethel clearly had changed her mind about him. She'd watched them hug. Knew what she saw. A woman clinging desperately to a man. And Finn holding her like he would never again let her go.

She must confront the situation head on. She pushed to her feet and went to the kitchen where her friends regarded her with pity. Well, they needn't bother feeling sorry for her. She would survive even if it meant packing up and going to find Ralph.

Finn and that woman sat in the dining room, their

heads close as they talked. The boy sat a distance away watching them. It had to be Eddie. She knew him to be seven, a year older than Kent, but he was smaller. Wore a wounded look. Jenny's heart went out to him.

She went to the outside door and called Kent. When he joined her, she said, "There's a little boy in the other room who looks so afraid and all alone. If Aunt Delcie agrees, maybe you could take him a toy and say hello."

Delcie nodded as Jenny thought she would. Delcie had a soft spot for all children, but especially those who seemed to be hurting.

Kent went to his bedroom and returned with two pieces of wood he'd picked up some time ago. One resembled a bear and the other a dog—if one had a vivid enough imagination. He paused at the doorway.

Delcie whispered in his ear. "Just say hello. Tell him your name and ask his. Remember how scary it is to be in a new place and not know anyone."

Kent crossed to Eddie's side. "'Lo. I'm Kent. What's your name?"

The other boy shuddered then croaked out his name. "Eddie."

"Wanna play?" Not waiting for an answer, Kent showed Eddie his pretend play animals. Soon the boys were sharing the toys and playing a game.

Eddie laughed. A deep, throaty sound that made Jenny smile.

Her smile fled as quickly as it came. She could imagine herself loving this child and giving him a home. A home she shared with Finn. Now that was not to be.

She allowed herself to look at Finn and the woman. Finn watched her, a question in his eyes. He signaled her to join him. She had faced Big Sam. She could surely face the man she had agreed to marry.

Hilda patted her back. "No need to look so fearful."

Jenny couldn't help it. She crossed the room and stood by the table.

"Jenny, this is Mrs. Hankins. Ethel, whom I have told you about. Ethel, meet Jenny Lyster. She's one of the women who own this establishment."

Not the woman he planned to marry. He couldn't have made his message any plainer. Jenny clung to her manners and greeted the woman. "Welcome to Willow Creek. Will you be staying long?"

Ethel looked at Finn as she answered. "Until things are settled."

"Can I get you anything else?" She nodded toward the empty coffee cups.

"We're fine. Unless you want something?" Ethel looked to Finn, a gentle smile creasing her mouth.

Finn shook his head.

"Enjoy your stay." Jenny hurried back to the kitchen and collapsed on the nearest chair. Her friends gathered around her.

"Vhat is going on?" Hilda asked.

"It's the woman he loves," she whispered, too shaken to speak louder. "That's her son. Finn and I were going to marry to give the boy a home." She explained about the letter and the odd request and how being pressed to marry because of their night in the hills seemed the perfect solution to all of it. "But now she's here and says she will stay." She lifted her pain-stinging eyes to her friends. "I think there will still be a wedding tomorrow, but it will be Finn and her."

"Why are you disappointed?" Delcie demanded. "You were being forced into the marriage. Now you are free. Oh wait, it still leaves you with your reputation in tatters."

Hilda fluttered her hand. "You miss vhat's really going on. Poor Jenny has fallen in love vith him."

Laura's face twisted. Tears clung to her lashes. "Oh Jenny. That's sad."

Little Sally came in from her play, saw the sad countenances on the women's faces, and her bottom lip came out and her eyes filled with tears.

Delcie scooped her up. "Don't you be upset. Everything is all right, sweet one."

"If she's staying, where will she stay?" Laura's question sent a shock through the room. They all knew the accommodations over at the run-down stopping house were not suitable for a woman.

"She can have my bed," Jenny said. "I'll share with Sally."

"Sally and Kent can share a bed," Delcie said.

"Are you sure about this?" Hilda asked.

"Are you all right?" Laura echoed.

"I'm fine. One does what one must."

"I vill tell her." Hilda hurried out of the room.

Jenny escaped outside. The little pine tree, that this morning had been a symbol of good things and the promise of more to come, mocked her with its presence. Bill watched as she hurried around the side of the shed and leaned against the wall. The mule trotted over and pressed his head to her shoulder.

She patted him, taking a tiny comfort in his presence.

Bill looked up and snorted, blowing his hot breath across Jenny's cheeks.

Finn stood by her. "We need to talk."

She wasn't prepared but would never be ready for this conversation. She might as well get it over with. "Agreed."

"Mrs. Meyer said Ethel could stay here as long as she needed."

"Yes."

"That was very kind of her." He twisted his fingers into Bill's tuft of hair that passed as a mane.

Jenny sucked in air and looked past Finn's left ear, afraid to meet his eyes for fear of saying more than she should. She emptied her heart of all the dreams and wishes and love that threatened to burst forth. "Finn, I won't marry you tomorrow."

"What? Why not? I thought we had this all settled."

She kept her gaze to his left. "That was before Ethel came. She's what you've always wanted. I won't stand in your way." She pushed past him and headed for the house.

Ethel was carrying her bags into Jenny's room, so Jenny veered to the side and went into Delcie's room. She stuck a chair under the doorknob so no one could enter then sank to the edge of Kent's bed. She'd be all right. She'd survive. Maybe she should join Ralph. Yes, that's what she'd do. As soon as she could find someone to take her to the fort,

Hilda knocked on the door. Delcie ordered her to open it.

Then a firmer knock. "Jenny, please open up. We must talk."

She ignored Finn's pleas. She couldn't face him until she had her emotions locked behind escape-proof doors.

18

Finn turned away from the door and faced the roomful of women who had shooed the children to the dining room, so they weren't spectators of this drama.

"She won't come out." His announcement was needless. Everyone could see for themselves.

"What happened?" Laura asked, her voice quivering.

"She said our wedding is off."

Delcie had her hands on her hips and fixed a hard look on him. "Are you marrying Ethel?" She nodded toward the woman who watched everything. No doubt confused by it all.

"Jenny seems to think I should." Was that the right thing to do? He could become Eddie's father and take care of Ethel. "Ethel, let's go for a walk. There are things to sort out."

He eyed Bill as they left the kitchen. The peace of his mountain cabin seemed mighty appealing at the moment. Then he shook his head. He needed to do what was best. But for who? For Ethel and Eddie? For Jenny? For himself?

Ethel spoke before he could gather a reasonable thought. "Finn, I regret saying that you had nothing to offer, but I had to clear up your misunderstanding of my kindness to you. I knew how unfair Father was in the way he treated the orphan boys he took in. All he cared about was the work he could get out of you and the others. I didn't think it was fair."

"But now you're without a husband and with a son to raise. I could help you." He swallowed hard. "I could marry you."

"Do you love me?"

Her question slammed into him like being hit with a wide board. What he felt for her paled in comparison to what he felt for Jenny. "I've always been fond of you. Always will be."

"Do you love that Jenny girl?"

"I...I guess I don't know." But even as he said those words, his cheeks warmed, his heart beat faster, harder, demanding. The truth lay in the depths of his encased heart. To say the words would require he let those walls crumble. Walls that had kept him safe all these years. Safe. Isolated. Lonely. Jenny had made him see that he was valued. That God loved him. That he was a mighty oak. Each remembrance chipped away a portion of those walls until they lay in dust.

"I love her." He almost shouted the words.

"Then you ought to tell her. By the way, I won't marry you, but thanks for asking."

"What will you do?"

"Finn, I have little time left. I want to see Eddie settled and happy. You will take him, won't you?"

He and Jenny had planned to give him a home. Would she still agree to it? "Of course."

"Thank you. I've explained to him about you and why I must do this. I want to go home to my parents. They would have kept Eddie but are both failing in health. I know they wouldn't be able to raise him to manhood."

She made it sound so final. Like she was going home to die. "But you look well."

"I took laudanum just before we arrived. It will soon wear off. I had hoped for a private place to sleep so I wouldn't disturb anyone. Unfortunately..."

Finn could think of no solution. But he'd ask Big Sam and Burnsie if they had any ideas.

They returned to the café. Finn looked at the closed bedroom door. He'd break it down if he must, but first things first. He gathered the women and explained what he planned to do then trotted over to the livery.

Big Sam listened carefully to Finn's explanation. "She can have my room. I'll sleep outside. I'll join you at your campsite so no one can think I might—" The big man scuffled his feet and looked away, embarrassed that people might think he'd do anything inappropriate.

"Sam, that isn't what I meant. I thought you might know someone nearby who would take in a boarder."

"She needs to be here, yes? To see to her son and all?"

"She wants to see him settled in his new life."

"Then my mind is made up. I'll clean my room now. You bring her over later." He jabbed his sausage-sized finger at Finn as he talked.

Finn agreed and returned to the café with his news. "I was afraid to say no. You know how Big Sam is."

Ethel looked both relieved and fearful. "It sounds ideal, but I hate to put the man out."

"He wouldn't take no for an answer," Finn said, but his attention was on the closed bedroom door. "Excuse me." He left the others and stood at the door. "Jenny, please open the door." He waited. Nothing. Though he might have heard the faintest sniffle. The sound swept away the last of the crumbling wall of his heart.

"Jenny, I'm not marrying Ethel. It's not what either of us wants."

More silence. He glanced back to see the four women watching him. He hesitated to speak the words overflowing from his heart before an audience. But they made no move toward leaving. The truth was, he didn't care if they heard what he had to say. Didn't care if the whole world did. There was only one person he hoped would hear. "Jenny, I'm not disappointed to not be marrying Ethel. I want to marry you and no one else."

He cocked his ear toward the door, hoping to hear her opening it.

Nothing.

He glanced back at the women. Mrs. Meyer and Ethel nodded encouragement. Delcie frowned and shook her head. Laura wrung her hands. Each had their opinion, but he didn't care if they approved or not.

He rattled the door, tried to push it open. Couldn't. "Jenny, I know you can hear me. I have so many things I want to tell you. Please let me say them to you."

The door didn't budge an inch.

Very well, he would say them to the door. "I want to give you a home and a family. Lots of children. A big house on a ranch." As he said it, he knew it was what he had always wanted. "I'll be the man running home to see you. Jenny, I love you."

His words were greeted by silence. Did no one in the room breathe? What more could he say to convince Jenny to open the door?

Perhaps the one thing he didn't want to say. "Jenny, it doesn't matter if you love me back or not."

Something on the other side of the door clattered and then the door flung open and Jenny burst out. "It's too late."

His heart sank to his feet.

"I already love you." She threw her arms around his neck.

"You do?" Did that surprised voice belong to him?

"Forever and always. Now kiss me."

He needed no more urging and right there in front of many witnesses, he kissed her thoroughly and soundly. He was loved. And he loved back. Was there ever a better feeling?

Giggles from the children ended their kiss.

He pulled Jenny to his side, his arm around her shoulders, and looked at Eddie.

"Eddie, I know your mama has told you what's happening and that she asked me to give you a home."

Ethel drew the boy toward Jenny and Finn. They squatted to his level.

Finn continued. "We would be proud for you to be our boy. I promise to love you and take care of you just as I would if you had been born to me. You'll have a place at the table with us."

Ethel pressed her hankie to her mouth. She'd seen how Finn was made to eat in a corner by himself, never invited to join the family.

Jenny touched the boy's shoulder. "You don't know us yet, but you'll learn that we want the best for you. I can imagine taking you on picnics, giving you school lessons, and reading you stories. Finn will teach you to ride and hunt and look after cows. How does that sound?"

Finn hoped the boy didn't hear only the dread of never-ending work. He would never use the boy in that way.

Eddie nodded. "It sounds good." He looked from

Jenny to Finn and smiled. "You kissed her in front of everyone."

"So I did. It's because I love her and want everyone to know."

"And I love him and don't mind showing it." Jenny grinned, her eyes full of emotion.

Eddie studied them both for a moment in which silence filled the room. "Maybe," he whispered, "you'll love me too."

Finn pulled the boy into an embrace. "You can count on it."

Jenny rubbed Eddie's back. Finn covered her hand with his and looked into her eyes. She blinked back tears.

Ethel sniffled, and she wasn't the only one.

Finn looked around the room. "Tomorrow Jenny and I will marry but today, at this very moment, we've become a family."

To his surprise and pleasure, the women clapped then crowded around them to congratulate them.

* * *

JENNY LOOKED at herself in the mirror as Laura arranged her hair in curls like a crown on her head.

"There you are. You're done. And you're beautiful."

"Thank you." But she and Finn shared a special secret. He saw her for more than her beauty just as she saw him for more than his ability to work.

Jenny stood to let Delcie and Laura look at her. She

wore her best dress—a pale green that made her eyes shine. Except she knew it wasn't the color that did that. It was her love for Finn.

"You are very fortunate," Delcie added. "To find a man who is honorable. I wish you all the best."

Those words coming from Delcie meant so much to Jenny. She hugged her friends. "Is Hilda ready?" Hilda was putting the finishing touches on a special lunch to be served after the ceremony.

Hilda stepped into the room. "It's time to begin. My, don't you look nice?"

"Thank you."

"Let's not keep the poor man vaiting." Hilda led the procession from the room. Jenny waited until they all left then paused before following. *Lord, I can't believe how You have blessed me. It's like what the Word says. 'All things work together for good to them that love God.'*

If she hadn't been hurt by how the Stanley men treated her, she would never have fled to the West and she wouldn't have met Finn.

The best thing to ever happen in her life.

She crossed the kitchen floor and paused at the doorway to the dining room. Where did all these people come from? She'd expected Burnsie and Big Sam. And Ethel, of course. The children watched curiously. She'd known they would be there. But Blaze and Emma? And so many others.

Finn smiled at her and she forgot everything else as she went to his side. He took her hand and pulled her close.

The Mountie read the wedding ceremony from a little black book.

"I now pronounce you husband and wife."

Finn didn't wait for the Mountie to say he could kiss the bride. He embraced her and kissed her so soundly her toes curled.

He slowly ended the kiss, his eyes holding hers, full of promises and dreams that they would fulfill together.

"No more walls," he whispered. "No more hiding on the mountain."

"I love you," she whispered back. "You are the man of my dreams."

A raucous roar came from outside. Bill stood with his face to the window, making his own peculiar sound.

Finn laughed. "Do you think he approves of what we've done?"

Bill blasted out another half whinny that ended in a hee-haw sound, and the crowd laughed.

What a great way to start their life together, Jenny thought. Humor, approval, shared joys, and wonderfully supportive friends. Her heart overflowed with love and gratitude. "God is so good."

"I truly feel like God is singing over us with joy."

"Me, too."

EPILOGUE

THREE MONTHS LATER.

*J*enny stood in the doorway of her home. A ranch house. Finn had been able to buy the ranch, along with the buildings and corrals, from a man whose wife was ill and needed to be taken back East where there was medical care for her. The house had been more than adequate, but Finn wasn't satisfied until the kitchen had been enlarged, a bay window put in the living room, and three bedrooms added on. He'd admitted to wanting a big family.

"Lots of love and laughter," he said.

Hilda had decided to add a room to the café for people who needed a decent place to stay. Before Jenny and Finn moved, it was their private room.

Finn had made a quick trip up to his cabin to get his belongings. He said he had no qualms about saying good-bye to the place.

The fence was finished, painted white with a row of wild roses in every hue of pink and red in front of it. And the garden had been bountiful. Jenny had helped can the peas and beans. She'd made a variety of pickles and relishes. The carrots, potatoes, turnips, and squash would be brought in before the freeze and stored in the root cellar Finn had made. It had been a good three months, but Jenny was eager to get on with life as Finn's wife and Eddie's mother.

With Eddie at her side, they watched Finn ride toward home. The boy was braver than Jenny could remember ever being. Ethel had prepared him as best she could for her leaving. But how does one prepare a child to say a final good-bye to his mother? Ethel had stayed a week, but it was evident to all that she was getting frailer. She didn't want Eddie to see her in her final days. Big Sam drove her to Fort Macleod and put her on the train. He was strangely quiet when he returned.

"I think he's grown fond of her," Jenny said. "The poor man must be lonely."

Delcie had snorted at her observation. "You don't have to be alone to be lonely."

Jenny smiled gently. "Someday, Delcie, someone will come along and make you forget the past and reach for the future."

"No need for that. I have the children."

After Ethel left, Eddie had tried to hide his pain until Jenny and Finn took him on a picnic and said they understood that he would miss his mama and that was all right. Finn told how frightened and angry he'd been when his parents died.

"We love you but know it will take time for you to learn to love us."

Eddie had broken down in sobs and thrown himself into Jenny's arms. She held him and comforted him. Finn sat beside them and wrapped his arms around them both. She stroked Eddie's hair and murmured softly, assuring him of their love. Finally, he had quieted but remained in her arms, spent by his tears.

The day marked a change in their relationship with him.

Bill played a big role in Eddie's adjustment. He followed the boy everywhere, touching him when he sensed Eddie was sad. He let Eddie climb on him and play about his feet. And now, Eddie was open and affectionate, though often cried over missing his mama.

They'd received news two weeks ago that Ethel had passed. The letter contained adoption papers making Jenny and Finn his legal parents. They had shown the papers to Eddie.

"It means you're forever our son," Finn said. "Here." He touched the paper. "And here." He put a hand to his heart.

Eddie's bottom lip quivered, and he ran to Jenny's

arms for comfort. Then climbed to Finn's lap and huddled there.

The boy was resilient and soon ran off to play with Bill.

That was the past. The future beckoned. Jenny and Eddie waited for Finn as he rode into the yard.

He left the horse at the barn and trotted across the yard toward her. Just like in her dream.

He hugged her then lifted Eddie and held him. "How are my two favorite people?"

"We're good now you're home," Jenny said, drawing him inside.

He shifted Eddie and reached into his pocket. "A letter for you."

She took it. "It's from Ralph." She tore it open, skimmed the page, and squealed. "He got married, and he's coming here so I can meet her, and he can meet you. And…" She lifted her face to Finn. "He says he'll find a place nearby so we can raise our families together."

"That's wonderful news."

"It's better than my dream." She kissed him. "You are everything I ever wanted."

Finn held her close. "And you are everything I never dared dream of."

DEAR READER

Thank you for reading A HEART'S YEARNING.

I often choose books based on reviews. If you liked this book or have comments would you please go to Amazon and leave a review so others can find it?

If you've enjoyed this story, and would like to read more of Linda's books, you can learn more about upcoming releases by signing up for her newsletter. You will also be able to download a free book, *Cowboy to the Rescue*. Click here to sign up.

Connect with Linda online:

Website | Facebook | Join my email newsletter

ALSO BY LINDA FORD

Buffalo Gals of Bonners Ferry series

Glory and the Rawhide Preacher

Mandy and the Missouri Man

Joanna and the Footloose Cowboy

Circle A Cowboys series

Dillon

Mike

Noah

Adam

Sam

Pete

Austin

Romancing the West

Jake's Honor

Cash's Promise

Blaze's Hope

Levi's Blessing

A Heart's Yearning

A Heart's Blessing

A Heart's Delight

A Heart's Promise

.

Made in United States
Troutdale, OR
10/21/2023